FORBIDDEN SECRETS

TERESA GABELMAN

ACKNOWLEDGMENTS

To everyone who has taken a chance on my stories and me, thank you. I wish I could name you all, but know I appreciate each of you so very much.

Becky Johnson, my editor, but more importantly my friend. Just because we are millions of miles away from each other, a day apart meant nothing when I needed you. The Facebook chat that we had, our face-to-face changed so much for me. I can never thank you enough for your understanding and for our true friendship. I needed that so very much at that moment and you gave it to me. I will never forget that day, that talk! I love and appreciate you more than you will ever know. When you tell me, "You got this!" I truly believe it! I do have this because of you.

CHAPTER 1

*L*eda sat in her car, staring at the restaurant where she used to work and prayed she wasn't making a big mistake. Glancing at herself in the rearview mirror, she adjusted the short blonde wig with a tug. Her money was running low, real low, and she needed to work. Glancing at her phone, which lay in the seat next to her, she knew she could pick it up and have help here within a day, but that wasn't an option. This was something she had to do on her own. It was her fight. She was doing it for not only herself and Sam, but her mother and father. She was going to get back what rightfully belonged to her and her brother.

After grabbing her sunglasses, she put them on, took one more glance at herself, then got out of the car. With each step she took toward the Red River Bar & Grill, her stomach tightened, and not because of the delicious aroma wafting to her nose. It tightened in fear of what could happen when she stepped through the door.

Her hand shook as she reached for the handle, then jumped out of the way as a customer came out at the same time she was going in. When he held the door open for her, Leda nodded her thanks, relieved she didn't know him.

Memories assaulted her as the door closed behind her and she stared at the place she had been so happy. Yes, she had loved her job here. Her eyes roamed, noticing everything looked the same as it had been the last time she had walked out, not realizing that would be her last time. Feeling the stares, she spotted an empty booth toward the back corner and headed that way. On busy days, customers would wait to be seated, but the sign was turned, indicating she could sit wherever there was a seat open.

With slow, easy steps, Leda reached the booth and sat down. Again, she was relieved because everyone seemed to go back to their food or conversation, not paying her much attention.

"I'll be with you in a sec," a familiar voice called out.

Leda glanced that way and tears stung the back of her eyes and clogged her throat. Jamie Lee, her best friend, hurried out of the back with a full tray loaded down with drinks. When she turned, Leda gasped. Jamie's, who was a year younger than herself, belly was swelled with child. She couldn't stop staring as Jamie made her way toward her.

"What can I get you to drink?" Jamie asked, standing at

her table, and Leda slowly looked up into her familiar face. The dark circles under her friend's once vibrant eyes were a stark contrast to her pale skin. "And go ahead and order if you're ready."

Not answering right away, Leda saw the irritation she knew so well light Jamie's tired eyes. Knowing Jamie didn't recognize her because of the wig and sunglasses she still wore, Leda made the decision to trust her once closest friend.

"A cherry Coke, without the cherry." She whispered the inside joke they had shared about old man Cooter, who always ordered a cherry Coke without the cherry.

Jamie looked away from her pad as her pencil stopped. Her skin paled even more, if that were possible, as tears wet her eyes. "No," she whispered, then shook her head. "You can't be here."

"But I am, and I'm not leaving." Leda glanced around to make sure no one was watching them before looking back up at Jamie. "Can I trust you?"

Reaching up, Jamie casually swiped a tear that escaped her eye. "With your life," she responded, then turned to get Leda's drink so as not to raise too much suspicion. Strangers anywhere raised some suspicion, but in a shifter town, everyone knew everyone, and if you weren't part of the pack, you were considered an enemy until cleared by the alpha. Her eyes roamed the restaurant. There were only a few faces she knew, and the rest were probably just people driving through, looking for a quick place to eat.

Placing the drink on the table, Jamie just gave her a nod

before going back to her other customers. Putting her lips to the straw, Leda took a drink and grinned as the taste of Coke and cherry filled her mouth. Pendleton County was only a day's drive from Beattyville, but as she sat there alone, it seemed much farther than that.

Her father, Jason Kingsman, had been a fair and just alpha to the Kingsman pack. He was feared, but well respected. Her mother, Jewel, had stood strong by her husband's side in all things. They had been a strong family that, in the end, had been devastated by someone her father trusted—his own brother, Allen.

Anger so pure, fresh, and overwhelming had her hands fisting tightly to the point she shook. Never had she felt such hatred for another being, whether human or shifter. Her father had welcomed his brother into their pack with open arms and was slaughtered for his trust by his own blood. If it hadn't been for her mother's quick thinking to send Leda and Sam away at the right time, then their family would have been wiped out completely. The memories assaulted her as she sat staring at nothing.

"But Momma," Leda said that fateful night, her voice shaking with fear as tears fell down her face. "I can't leave you."

"Leda, you dry those tears right this minute." Her mother hissed the whisper as she hurried them down through the basement, then opened the secret door that no one other than they knew about. She pushed both Leda and Sam through the door and grabbed Leda's arm. "You take Sam and run. Don't you dare look back, you hear me?"

The heavy pounding footsteps above their heads made her

mother's grip tighten. Leda could only nod as she looked from the ceiling back to her mother.

"Your job is to keep Sam safe." Her mom finally let go of her arm as she knelt and pulled a crying Sam into her arms. "I love you, Sam. You listen to your sister, you hear me?"

Sam sniffed, hugging his mother tightly around the neck. "I lo-lo-love—"

He was cut off by the sound of the basement door crashing open. Her mom pushed them deeper through the door and grabbed Leda in a tight hug. "I love you," she whispered, then pulled away, and Leda knew her mom was ready to shift. Her eyes swirled, but her mother was holding on to make sure they got away. "Promise me you will never try to avenge your father or me."

It was a promise Leda couldn't make. She gasped when growls and footsteps echoed toward them. Wolves and men were coming, and they were coming fast.

"Promise me," her mother urged as she backed up toward the door. Leda opened her mouth, but before she could speak, her eyes met her mother's before she slammed the door, then heard the shelves being pulled down over it to conceal its identity.

Leda reached out, her scream of frustration stuck in her throat. She quietly knelt, took Sam's hands and placed them over his ears, putting a finger to her lips for him to remain silent. He nodded before squeezing his eyes shut. Knowing they had to go, she picked Sam up and, as quickly as she could, hurried through the tunnel her father had made for an escape. It was something they had been drilled on, but never in her life did she think it would ever have to be used.

The sounds of fighting and shrill screams of pain echoed toward them. Tears fell hard and fast, blurring her vision through the darkness of the tunnel. Her eyesight was better than any human's, but with the tears, it was almost impossible.

Suddenly, the screams stopped, and, at that point, she knew. Dropping to her knees, Leda held Sam tightly against her as she mourned for her mother and father in the coldness of the tunnel.

Leda jumped as a plate was placed in front of her. BLT and golden french fries replaced her vision of sorrow. Glancing up at Jamie, she knew her friend had gone ahead and placed her order without Leda saying a word. She wanted so badly to talk to her like they always did, but the danger was too great.

Jamie once again walked away to wait on other customers. Leda did her best to finish all the food, not knowing when the next meal would come. She was almost out of money, not having much to begin with, and needed to use it sparingly. She had been gone from Lee County for almost a week, staying in a cheap motel and making her plans for what she was about to do. The one constant she knew was she needed help.

Glancing back at Jamie's belly, she realized that asking Jamie for help wasn't something she could do. Risking her friend's life was bad enough, but risking her unborn child was quite simply not going to happen.

Hearing motorcycles, she glanced toward the window to see three men ride up. She looked at Jamie, who was hurrying toward her.

"You have to get out of here," Jamie hissed, then laid her bill down, making sure Leda saw an address written on the back. Leda slipped it into her pocket and took the other bill Jamie discreetly laid down as she took her plate.

Before Leda could get up, the men were already inside, their voices booming above everyone else. She also noticed that no one was looking at them. It had grown silent except for them. None of them were familiar to her, and definitely none were her uncle.

As Jamie walked by, a man with a long beard grabbed her around the waist, pulling her to him and almost upsetting the plate from her hand. "Hey, babe," he said loudly as he kissed her in front of everyone, then rubbed her belly. "How about getting us some drinks and food."

"Sure, Minor," Jamie replied as she pulled away. "Just let me put this plate in the back first."

"Well hurry the hell up," he grouched, his frown replacing the smirk he had worn. "We're hungry and ready to eat."

Minor? What kind of name is that? Leda thought, not liking the man instantly. She quickly glanced away as the man looked around at everyone, but his eyes went right past her as if she weren't there as he sat with the other two men.

She gained courage; if she didn't know them, they sure as hell wouldn't know her. They may have seen pictures of her from when Allen was hunting her and Sam down, and was probably still hunting them, but with her wig and sunglasses, there was no way they would know who she was.

Standing, she walked toward the register and waited. Jamie came out with four drinks. "Let me give these guys their drinks, and I'll be right there," Jamie said as she would have to any other customer.

"Take your time," Leda replied, lying through her teeth. She wished to hell she would hurry because she needed to get the hell out of there. But they were playing roles, and she was thankful Jamie was on her side.

Jamie hurried over, took the bill without the address on it, and rang her up. "That will be eight seventy-five."

Leda handed her a ten, then gave her a nod. "Keep the change."

"Keep the change." Minor, who was watching, frowned. "Bullshit. My girl gave you service and deserves more than a three-dollar tip."

More like a dollar twenty-five, dumbass, she wanted to say, but noticed now that everyone was looking at her. She reached in her pocket, grabbed the five she knew was there, and handed it to Jamie, who had remained silent throughout the whole thing.

"Now that's more like it." The man snorted and gave her a glare before going back to talking to his friends, who were probably just as big of assholes as he was.

Jamie and Leda shared a look before she turned around and walked out of the restaurant. The cool breeze felt so good she gulped in a deep breath, letting it fill her lungs that wanted to let loose a scream of revenge.

CHAPTER 2

*T*az sat inside a small diner drinking coffee. Glancing at his watch, he frowned, all too aware he was wasting time sitting here. He had already wasted a week being a self-centered prick while Leda could be in trouble. He cursed, drawing a few curious stares from an older couple having breakfast at the table beside him.

When Taz had found out that Leda was planning on leaving the pack to search for her father, he had left immediately to find her. Their conversation hadn't gone as he planned, however; it never did where she was concerned. He was and had always been deeply in love with her, but he wasn't sure she felt the same about him. He knew there were feelings just by her actions, but she was younger than him. Not by much in age, but in world experiences, he felt ancient next to her.

She'd blown him off when he offered to help find her

father. He was the most skilled tracker, but she had flat-out refused him. The more he'd tried, the more she'd stepped back from him, as if wanting to put as much distance between them as possible. That had hurt, a lot. It also hurt his pride knowing the woman he wanted didn't want him. Her actions screamed the truth.

And then to discover she had lied set him on the brink of insanity. Knowing she was out there ready to face down the alpha of what used to be her father's pack in order to avenge her parents' death had every protective instinct he possessed screaming inside his body.

He had to find her.

Glancing back at his watch, he snarled. He would give the asshole five more minutes and no more; then he was gone.

"Refill?" The waitress came up with a freshly brewed pot of coffee.

"Thank you." Taz nodded, not paying attention to the woman's stare as she poured the coffee.

"You sure I can't get you anything to eat?" she asked after his cup was filled to the rim. "We are famous for our breakfast."

"I'm good." Taz wasn't much for small talk, never had been. Seeing the disappointment on the older woman's face, he felt bad. "But thank you. It does smell great, but coffee is all I need this morning."

Okay, that was probably more than he had said in the last week to anyone, but the woman's smile made it worth it. He knew she was just being motherly, at least that was how it felt to him. The truth was he couldn't bear to eat; his appetite had vanished the minute he found out Leda had slipped out of town.

Glancing out the window, he scanned the area. She was out there somewhere, and not knowing if she was safe or in danger was driving him insane. Taz had always been a loner, even as a child. He had to grow up fast, providing for his mother and sister when their father up and left with no word. It wasn't until years later that his father showed back up thinking he could pick up where he left off, which wasn't saying much. He was a drunk who depended on his wife to earn a living. He'd never laid a hand on him or his sister; he'd never seen him hit his mother, even though he had questioned the bruises she tried to hide. But Taz heard the mental abuse, lived it himself from his father.

"You're a good-for-nothing breed," his father would slur during his binges. His father, Cusa Azure, full-blood Cherokee, his mother a beautiful Irish angel who his father threw away. Though always after the binges and mental abuse, his mother would find him.

"Your name means Gift of God." Her words, spoken in her soft Irish accent, would tell him what a wonderful man he would become and that he already was. Aileen had been a beautiful soul who he loved more than anything and missed with every fiber of his being. "And you are my gift from God. You are kind, thoughtful of others, and strong. You will be a skillful warrior one day, and that, my amazing son, is how I raised you."

It was her words he hung onto for years, up until this day, and yet there were times his father's voice would

11

seep into his mind. He swore not only to himself but to his mother that he would not let her down. Taz knew her spirit was with him and he damn sure would make her proud. He refused his father's last name. Instead, he'd taken his mother's—Whelan, meaning wolf. She gave him the use of her surname on her deathbed. Both the Cherokee and Irish took great pride in their names and meanings. He was no different. A smirk played on his lips as his eyes darkened, thinking of the meaning to his father's name: the one who provokes. How fitting for the bastard.

After his mother had died, Taz and his sister left while their father was passed out in his chair. With only the clothes on their backs and what he stole from his father's wallet, they were on their own. His sister was two years older than him, but he took the role of care-giver, decision-maker, and did a damn good job of it. They found a pack who accepted them. The alpha fell in love with his sister in spite of their seven-year age difference, and Taz approved after months of seeing Dawn would be well taken care of. And now he was doing what he promised his mother—trying to make it in a world that was against his kind just to make her proud. He would not fail in life, and he would die before he failed Leda.

A sick feeling hit him. He had let his pride prevent him from immediately going out to find Leda, but if he'd known she was walking toward trouble, he would not have let her out of his sight.

Downing the rest of his coffee, he tossed a twenty down on the table, knowing it would pay his bill and leave a good tip, and then made to stand. He'd waited long enough.

"Guess you're really in a bind if you called me for help." Steve's voice made him pause.

Taz looked toward the door as Steve made his way to the table and sat down across from him.

"So, Mr. Tracker Extraordinaire, what can I help you with?" Steve leaned back in his chair as if he had all day, his arms crossed over his chest.

Okay, so most thought he hated Steve, and actually, he kind of did. No, he really did. But Taz also knew Leda and Steve had a history, one he wanted to kill the vampire over, but wouldn't... yet.

"Has she contacted you?" Taz tried not to snarl the question, but it couldn't be helped. Knowing Leda held feelings for the asshole made his wolf rage and the man seethe with anger.

"Maybe," Steve countered, still looking composed. He then leaned toward the table. "That question could have easily been answered over text. So why meet, Tax?"

His instinct was to tear the bastard's throat out, but he refrained and instead leaned toward him, his eyes dark with rage. "Listen and listen good, vamp. I don't like you. You don't like me."

Steve snorted in agreement, but other than that didn't comment.

"Me not coming across this table to tear your fucking throat out is not an act of kindness, so don't mistake it for such." Taz's voice lowered dangerously. "The only matter in this moment is Leda."

"Couldn't agree more." Steve hadn't backed away one inch during Taz's snarled speech. "Do you have a plan, or are we just going to sit here and see who has the bigger balls, because honestly, I'd win that fucking war. You drew first blood the day I met you, fucker. But for Leda, I will put my hatred for you behind me. So truce until Leda is found and safe, agreed?"

Taz looked at Steve's outstretched hand, then back at Steve as he grasped the vampire's hand in a handshake that lasted longer than it should have, each man squeezing to the point of pain on each side.

"Ah, boys." The waitress cleared her throat as she stared at their clasped hands. "How about breaking that up and I'll get you some more coffee?"

Taz let go as soon as he felt Steve's grip loosen. This union was going to try every ounce of patience he possessed, but he knew that if Leda contacted someone, it would be this asshole, and he wanted to be sure he was there when that happened if they didn't find her first.

"What's the plan?" Steve asked as he dumped half of the sugar from the glass container in his cup. Taz made a disgusted face as he watched. He liked his coffee black and strong, not black and syrupy.

"You seriously going to drink that?" Taz watched as Steve lifted it to his mouth and took a long gulp.

"Yep." Steve sat it down, then added more sugar as if to spite Taz.

Jesus, this was going to be harder than he thought. Taz glanced around to make sure no one was close enough to hear them. "I told Garrett and them to hang back."

"Oh, and how did that go over?" Steve smirked, taking another drink of coffee. This time he made a disgusted face, making Taz grin.

"Not well, but after I explained my plan, they agreed," Taz replied, glancing at his watch again.

"Did it take you this long to tell them the plan?" Steve asked in his normal smartass manner. "Because Jesus, man, let's get to it already."

Taz ignored his remarks. "Garrett knew Leda's father from a long time ago."

"Yeah, Sloan said Hunter told him Leda was thought to be going looking for her dad, but Sam let it out that their uncle had killed both their mom and dad." Steve's eyes darkened with anger. "Bastard."

"Yeah, and the last place he knew the pack to reside is Pendleton County," Taz added, finally leaning back, trying to relax, but the more time wasted talking about it meant Leda could be suffering. "She's going to fight for her pack against her uncle."

Steve's eyes narrowed as he slammed his hand on the table. "Okay, that's new fucking information."

"Garrett said this is your territory," Taz continued,

ignoring Steve's small outburst. "If the pack still resides in this area and we go in there as a pack, then shit will hit the fan. But if I go in with you, it won't seem as if it's much of a threat. Just a shifter and a vampire passing through."

Steve thought for a minute, then nodded. "Ah, and you don't think people will notice that?"

Taz shrugged as he looked away from Steve to the patrons inside the small diner. "I'm willing to take that chance." He glanced back at Steve. "Are you?"

Steve stood, draining the last bit of coffee and tossing another twenty on the table. "Ready when you are, *Tax.*"

Yeah, it was going to be really hard not to kill the son of a bitch, but right now, he needed the asshole.

Shaking his head, Taz followed Steve outside and headed for his bike. If worse came to worse, he'd offer Steve up as a trade.

Another rare smile lit his face but didn't quite reach his eyes.

CHAPTER 3

*L*eda stopped on the old dirt road, glanced at the
address Jamie gave her and frowned. Where in
the hell was she sending her? She slowly crept
down the road, if you could even call it that, her eyes on
the house straight ahead. She knew this old road, actually knew the house now that she was here. What she
didn't know was who lived there. Surely Jamie wouldn't
send her to her own house, since her friend about had a
heart attack when that asshole showed up at the restaurant. He must be part of her uncle's men for Jamie to
panic as she had.

Pulling into the driveway, which was in bad shape, holes
and dips bottomed out her car as she pulled up. She
cursed. Leda definitely could not afford for anything to
happen to her car. Stopping, she just sat staring, not
really sure what to do. There were no cars around. No

one was inside that she could tell. Shutting the car off, she took the keys and tucked them into her pocket.

Opening the door, she stepped out but left the door open just in case she needed to make a fast getaway. Glancing at the driveway, Leda knew that would be next to impossible for any kind of speed on the uneven surface.

With measured steps and her senses alert, she moved toward the porch that had seen better days. One fold-up chair sat against the house with a small table and a beer can on top. Cigarette butts littered the overgrown yard, and she stopped when she noticed one still smoldering in the glass at the edge of the porch. Someone was here.

Her eyes flew to the porch as the door opened.

"Who the fuck are you and what do you want?" a man snarled, and as he stepped farther out onto the porch, her heart soared.

"Malcolm," she whispered as she took in his gaunt appearance. Jamie's older brother had always been her idol. Leda absolutely adored him, but seeing him like this broke her heart. His eyes looked haunted, and there was a silent rage burning deep inside them.

"I asked you a question!" He grabbed a rifle from inside the door but didn't aim it—yet.

Leda had no idea who to trust, but if Jamie hadn't turned her over at the restaurant and instead sent her here, then maybe she should trust him. Yet uncertainty had her second-guessing. Seeing him like this, she wasn't sure. "Jamie sent me."

"Why the hell would she do that?" Malcolm swiped his

long black hair from his eyes. "She lives with that piece of shit, not here. So go on, get." He waved his hand at her as if shooing a fly.

Not knowing what to do, she turned to leave but stopped. Turning her head, Leda really looked past his crude dismissal of her to see the friend she once knew. Had her parents' death and her disappearance done this to him? Needing to know the truth before she disappeared, she put it all on the line.

"Make me," she said, loud enough for him to hear. When his head tilted slightly in recognition, she added, "Mally."

"Jesus." His whisper reached her ears. "Leda?"

She nodded slowly, turning back around. "Yeah, it's me." She stayed where she was. "Are you friend or foe, Malcolm?"

He was off the porch and in front of her before she could blink. He wrapped her in his arms and squeezed the breath out of her. "I thought they'd killed you. We all did." He held her even tighter, then pulled back. "Sam?"

"Safe." Tears burned the back of her eyes.

He nodded, then hugged her again before pulling her toward the house. "Come on." He rushed her up the steps and inside, closing the door behind him.

Reaching up, she pulled off her wig and took off her sunglasses. Scratching her head with one hand and tossing the wig on an old kitchen table, she glanced up at Malcolm, who was staring at her as if he were watching a ghost. "I'm real, Malcolm."

He shook the dazed look off his face. "I can't believe it." He sat down heavily at the table, still staring at her. "How in the hell did you get away? And why in the fuck did you come back to this hell, Leda? Are you crazy?"

Malcolm had no clue how many times she'd asked herself on the way there. "Yeah, maybe." She shrugged. "The tunnels in the old house. Mom sent us through just before…." She couldn't finish. Didn't have to. Everyone knew exactly what happened to her parents, but in their world, no authorities were called. The only justice to be served would be by her hand.

"I'm so damn sorry." Malcolm pushed his hair from his face as his head dropped. "I should have fought that son of a bitch before he could…. *Fuck!*" Malcolm stood, grabbed an empty beer bottle and threw it against the wall.

"No one saw this coming," Leda said after a few seconds of silence. "There was no way you could have known, and if you had fought, you would have been killed, leaving Jamie alone."

His bitter laugh rang throughout the small house. "Oh, I did her a real solid," he spat in disgust. "She's a whore to that bastard, Minor, and knocked up with his kid."

"I'm sorry." Leda didn't know what else to say. Maybe she had waited too long. Maybe she shouldn't have run. If she had been a boy at her age, then it would have been expected of her to stay and right the wrong her uncle did to their family.

Malcolm shook his head as he looked at her. "You have to get out of here." He was frantic in his statement as he glanced at the door. "By now they know a stranger is here. If Allen even thinks you're Leda Kingsman, you'll be dead before the sun goes down."

"I'm not leaving, Malcolm." Leda stood her ground. "I will leave this house so you're not involved, but I'm here and I'm not going anywhere."

"Why?" His eyes were wide with disbelief. "Why in the hell would you want to be anywhere near this place?"

"He took not only the lives of my parents, but he also took what rightfully belongs to me and my brother." Leda's voice was strong and sure, but deep inside, fear rode her hard. Despite being terrified, determination kept her steady. "And I'm here to get it back."

The room was silent, almost to the point that her ears rang as Malcolm just stared at her. She needed numbers on her side. Leda felt she could count Jamie as one since she didn't turn her over and sent Leda to her brother. She hoped she could count Malcolm as two.

"Shit!" he finally said, then walked to the refrigerator, grabbing a beer. He offered her one, but she refused. He slammed the door shut, twisted the cap off and drank more than half before removing it from his lips. "So where in the hell have you been?"

Taking that as a good sign, she sat at the table with a sigh of relief. "Everywhere." Leda looked around the house. There were a lot of empty beer bottles and cans scattered around the place. Her heart tightened with sadness thinking Malcolm had somehow lost hope. And maybe he had, but she was here to change that, even if it meant giving her life. She owed her father and mother that sacrifice, as well as Sam.

"They looked for you everywhere, but then we heard nothing." Malcolm's eyes turned haunted. "We figured you were dead. Only Allen's men were allowed to search for you because the bastard knew any one of us would help you and Sam. But Allen failed, didn't he? He didn't find you?"

"Came close a few times, but we were able to get away." Leda frowned at the memories. She would love to forget them, but she couldn't. She refused to let them go because it was her driving force to take back the Kingsman pack. "We had a rough road for a while, but then we met up with a woman who was searching for her father. Sam and I both took to her, and then we ended up being part of the Lee County wolves pack."

"Lee fucking County wolves?" Malcolm's eyes lit up.

"Ah, yeah," Leda replied, then grinned. "Why?"

"Where in the hell are they?" Malcolm sat up straighter. "They could come in here and wipe Allen and his bitches out! We saw that Hunter guy working with the VC Warriors on television. Saw him shift and shit. Are you kidding me? Seriously, where in the hell are they?"

"This is my fight," Leda replied, realizing Malcolm was not going to understand. She was right. He slapped his hand hard across his forehead and glared at her as if she'd lost her mind. "I will not bring anyone innocent into this fight, Malcolm. They have families and—"

"I don't give a rat's ass if they've got a dozen rug rats

and a granny rocking on the front fucking porch." Malcolm finished his beer, then went to get another one. "The Lee fucking County wolves."

She rolled her eyes. "Yes, the Lee fucking County wolves," she mocked.

"What, didn't they like you or something?" Malcolm looked at her thoughtfully, as if not believing she didn't involve them in this.

"They liked me just fine." Leda frowned with narrowed eyes. "What's not to like?"

"You were always a pain in the ass." Malcolm saluted her with his beer. "So I thought maybe, just maybe, you weren't the *dumbass* I was thinking you are by not involving them and that they just didn't like you enough to help you."

Leda snorted. "Everybody likes me."

The room became silent again as they both thought the same thing. "Not everyone," Malcolm voiced what they both knew. "As long as you and Sam are alive, Allen is not the rightful alpha to this pack. The Kingsman was set up differently than other packs to protect it for Sam."

"Or me," Leda added, knowing the reaction she was going to receive. Though his laughter was not really the one she thought she'd get.

"A woman can't be alpha of a pack, Leda," he replied after his laughter died down. When she didn't respond, he became serious. "A woman cannot be alpha."

"Who says?" Leda shot back, then crossed her arms over her chest as she leaned back.

Okay, that stumped him since he looked a little confused. "How the hell should I know? But I know they can't, and that's that."

"No, that's not that's that," she replied with a huff. "If I beat Allen Kingsman fair and square, the pack is mine."

Malcolm let out a long breath as he stared at her. "You really believe you can beat your uncle for the pack?"

"Yes, in time, I do." Leda didn't even blink or look away as she answered that question. What she wasn't saying was that even though she would most probably be killed, her uncle would die right next to her by her hand, and vengeance would be hers and Sam's. If she had to die, then so be it. The day she ran through the tunnels holding her brother in her arms, she'd made a vow knowing that even succeeding in revenge would mean her death. She had made peace with that.

A sudden image of Taz floated at the edge of her mind, but she pushed it away. Nothing and no one would stand in her way of the vow she'd made the night her world was shattered.

CHAPTER 4

*B*efore Taz and Steve could leave the parking lot of the restaurant, they were already arguing. "Dude, if you go blowing in there on that bike, you're going to draw attention that we don't need."

"I'm not leaving my bike," Taz replied without looking Steve's way. "And I'm not riding in that fucking minivan."

"What's wrong with my minivan?" Steve frowned, looking at it. "It's multifunctional. Family car by day, Warrior van by night. I can carry weapons and Warriors comfortably. No one expects a van full of badass Warriors to roll up and pile out. I call that a win."

"Call it what you want. I'm still not riding in it." Taz straddled his bike and glanced at the damn van with disgust.

"Yeah, well, once you start having little pups running

around, you'll change your mind." Steve snorted knowingly.

"Do you ever shut the hell up?" Taz growled, rubbing his tired eyes.

"Ah…." Steve seemed to think about it. "No."

"How far are we?" Taz asked through teeth clenched so hard he swore he heard one crack.

Before Steve could answer, his phone rang. He held up his finger as he answered it. "Yo."

Taz knew he was going to strangle the son of a bitch before the day was over. His fingers actually itched at the thought. All he wanted was to find Leda, make sure she was safe, and take her back home where she belonged—by his fucking side. Yeah, this tiptoeing shit around the issue of her being his was over.

Steve's words on the phone drew his attention.

"Is she in danger?" Steve's voice changed from dumbass to serious in one breath.

Taz about came off the bike, but Steve gave him a thumbs-up. What the fuck did that even mean? Thumbs-up she was okay? Or thumbs-up she was in danger, and they were leaving so he could kill someone?

"Yeah." Steve nodded, even though he was on the phone. "I got this. No, we aren't waiting. Like I was telling Tax…"

Taz's fingers itched again, and he actually pictured them around Steve's throat.

"...the less attention we draw to ourselves the better until we know what's going on." Steve glanced at Taz. "No, he's calm. I told him how it was."

Taz flipped him off with a snarl. He was seriously rethinking his decision to have Steve involved.

The vamp finally hung up, taking his time putting his phone in his pocket before saying anything.

"That was Hunter," Steve said as he looked around the parking lot they still stood in. "Some guy called the Warriors saying Leda was with him."

Anger and relief swarmed his body, his eyes narrowed. "Where?" was the only word growled from his lips.

"Hold on, chief." Steve shook his head. "We can't go barreling into town. This guy, Malcolm, said there are eyes everywhere. He said we have to wait until night, but she's safe for now."

One thing about Taz was he didn't take orders well when it came to Leda. He wanted her by his side now. "Call me that one more time," he warned, his eyes narrowing dangerously.

"Listen, Tax," Steve continued to push his buttons, "I'm here for Leda. I don't give a rat's ass if you like me or not."

Taz took a deep calming breath, counted to ten, and when that didn't help his rage, he counted again and took another deep calming breath. "Where. Is. She?"

"Hunter texted me the address, but we aren't going anywhere until you agree to park the damn bike before we get into town." Steve crossed his arms and leaned against the van. "You know I'm right, but you're too damn hardheaded to admit it."

Slowly, Taz got off his bike and walked straight up to Steve until they were nose-to-nose. He had to give Steve credit; the guy just stood there staring at him. "I don't like you," Taz said, his eyes narrowing. "Don't think you're calling the shots."

"Actually, I am calling the shots, because I'm not thinking with my heart or my dick." Steve's voice remained level, not loud or quiet, just calm and cool. "I'm happily married to the woman who owns my heart. I love Leda, but not in the way you have confused. She is my sister who no one will hurt, including you. So think what you want, but you know I'm right. Leave the fucking bike."

Taz heard his words, and to his surprise, he believed him. Go figure. His thinking where Leda was concerned was always a bit clouded. He also knew Steve was actually right. His bike would draw attention, but he sure as fuck didn't want to admit that to Steve.

"Okay, but just let me say—" Steve thought for a moment with a weird look on his face. "—when I kissed Leda, she wasn't like a sister to me because that would have just been weird."

"I'll find a place to stash the bike." Taz turned around and got back on his bike before he punched Steve in the mouth. "How far and what way?"

Glancing at his phone, Steve frowned. "About forty-five

minutes from here and turn left, then south on the AA Highway."

Taz gave a nod, then started his bike without saying a word.

"Ya know, I think if you get that stick out of your ass, we could be friends." Steve opened the van door, calling out over his shoulder, "I'm not only a pretty funny guy, hilarious actually, but I'm also as fucking loyal as they come."

Revving his bike, Taz ignored him as he took off, following Steve's directions. What pissed him off was Steve was probably right. If Taz didn't have the ever-present chip on his shoulder, they probably could be friends.

Then again, hearing he had kissed Leda had Taz wanting to tear his throat out. Maybe friends was stretching it a bit.

~

Leda lay on the couch watching a *Friends* marathon. Malcolm had something to do, so he'd left her alone with rules and warnings. "Don't leave, don't answer the door, don't go outside," so on and so forth. She made the smartass remark that he needed to write them down because no way could she remember them all.

Reaching around, she pulled out her phone and turned it on. Immediately alerts for texts sounded. She had over fifty unread messages. Scrolling through them, she saw one from Steve. Opening it, she grinned and felt her eyes tear up.

You missed my wedding. I expect a damn good reason and an amazing gift. Love and miss you, dog breath. Call me ASAP!

Wiping a tear, she continued to scroll without opening any until Taz's messages began. When she opened the last one, her stomach clenched in anticipation.

Why didn't you come to me? If I don't hear from you in the next hour, I will come and find you. I will find you, Leda.

Sitting straight up, she gasped. They knew. Sam blabbed. She couldn't blame her brother; he was probably scared and worried. He was so young, too young to be going through what they'd been through. She hated putting any of this on Sam, but they had talked about this before they had ever met the Lee County wolves. It had only been the two of them for so long.

She read the text again and knew without a doubt that Taz would make good on his text, which was sent a day ago. There was nothing else from him.

Panic started to settle in as she stood and paced, staying away from the windows. She didn't want anyone involved. It was too dangerous. Considering her uncle killed his own brother, he would easily kill anyone else who stood in his way or threatened what he wanted to keep, which was obviously the Kingsman pack. God, how she hated the man. To even think she was blood-related to the bastard made vomit rise to her throat.

This was her business, no one else's. She didn't even like bringing in Malcolm and Jamie, but she needed a little help on the inside. Soon, she would be back on her own; she just needed more information before she set her plan in action.

A knock on the door had her jumping and then running to hide. Reaching up to make sure her wig was in place, she held her breath as the door opened. Dammit, she should have been paying more attention. If she had any hope of avenging her parents and taking over the pack, she needed to get her shit together.

"Malcolm? Leda?" Jamie's voice called out in a whisper as the door shut.

Leda came around the corner of the kitchen into the living room. "You scared me to death."

"Good!" Jamie frowned, putting a bag on the table just past the door. "What in the hell are you thinking, Leda? You were free from this hellhole. What are you doing back? And where's Malcolm?"

"He said he had something to take care of and he'd be right back," Leda replied, then glanced down at her friend's stomach. "Boy or girl?"

"I don't know." Jamie rubbed her belly lovingly, but the sadness on her face broke Leda's heart. "I haven't been to a doctor yet. Minor said I didn't need to see a doctor, that women have babies every day, so I need to suck it up. Be a woman, he says."

"He's one of my uncle's men?" Leda asked, already knowing the answer to that question.

Jamie nodded as she went to a chair and sat down, putting her swollen feet up on the coffee table. "Yeah."

"I'm sorry." Leda sighed, sitting across from Jamie.

"What are you sorry for?" Jamie kicked off her shoes and wiggled her toes. "None of this is your fault. Seriously, Leda, what are you doing back here? We didn't know if you got away or if you'd been killed."

"He's not getting away with what he did." Leda lifted her head proudly.

"Honey, he already did." Jamie's response wasn't meant to be mean. Just the facts. "He got away with all of it, and he's still getting away with it. You are not going to be able to stop him."

"Let me worry about that," Leda replied, not wanting to let Jamie know how far she was willing to go to see her uncle defeated.

The door opened, making both of them jump and gasp.

"Dammit, Malcolm." Jamie leaned back after seeing it was her brother. "Knock next time."

"It's my house," Malcolm replied, grabbing the bag that Jamie had set on the table. He walked over and kissed Jamie on the top of the head. "So, prego, what's for dinner?"

"Chicken soup, club melt, and onion rings." She leaned her head back, closing her eyes. "You might need to nuke it."

Leda watched Malcolm and Jamie, her heart dropping to her stomach. What in the hell was she doing here putting them in danger? If her uncle even got a hint that they helped her, they'd pay dearly.

Before she could say anything, Malcolm cursed at the sink in the kitchen. Looking that way, she saw him staring out the window before he turned toward her, his face a mask of panic and fear.

"Hey, beggars can't be choosers or however that goes." Jamie mistook his curse, thinking it was because of what she brought for him to eat.

"Minor," Malcolm said as he rushed into the living room.

Before any of them could react, the door opened, and Minor's eyes went straight to Leda. "What the fuck is she doing here?"

CHAPTER 5

*T*az sat in the passenger seat of Steve's fucking minivan wondering if instead of some back road in Kentucky, he was on the road to Hell. Steve talked nonstop, knowing Taz would rather gut him than speak one word to him, and yet the guy didn't seem to care. He was talking like they were old friends. What in the actual hell was going on?

Glancing at his phone, he knew while Leda hadn't responded to his texts, he had hoped the last one would draw a reaction from her. It hadn't. After Steve's phone call with Hunter, he at least knew she was okay, for now.

He stared out the window. They were close. Taz needed to get control of his emotions and play this right. Leda's life depended on it. Watching the trees fly by, a small smile curved his lips as he wondered if these woods were where Leda grew up. Had she let her wolf run this land? He was sure she had. There was so much he didn't know about her, and yet he felt as if he'd known her forever.

The first time Taz had seen Leda, his wolf had taken immediate notice, and so had the man. From that moment, she had been his, whether she knew it or not. Apparently though, she hadn't known it since she seemed to fight him every step of the way. Either that or she was in denial.

He knew Garrett and the rest were stumped on why he had let her walk away. He hadn't known she was walking into danger. If he had, Taz never would have allowed that. At least he wouldn't have allowed her to go into this alone, but he had never forced anyone to do anything against their will. If she had wanted to stay with him, she would have. It had taken everything he possessed just to stand silently as she'd left, but he'd known he would find her again once she'd found what she was in search of. Unfortunately, he hadn't known it was revenge against the bastard who'd killed her parents.

"Hey, dude." Steve's voice brought him out of his thoughts.

"What?"

"Listen, man, I know we didn't get off on the right foot," Steve began as Taz sighed, rubbing his eyes, "but just know that I would lay my life down for Leda, not because I want her, but because she's special."

Taz didn't brush his words aside as he usually did with Steve. Instead, he heard the truth in them. How could he hate someone who had his woman's best interest at heart? Dammit, he had been such a bastard to this guy and yet here he was, driving a fucking minivan into a possible battle that wasn't really his. He had just gotten married, left his new bride to help him find Leda. Taz felt like a total dick. He *was* a dick, who was he kidding?

"She is," Taz agreed, then cleared his throat. "Congrats on your marriage, man."

"Thank you," Steve answered, without saying more, which was a total shocker.

"I appreciate, ah, you know..." Taz tripped over the nice words. "...you, ah, being here and... shit."

"That was a fumbled mess." Steve snorted with a chuckle, glancing over at Taz. "I bet that was the hardest damn thing you've ever had to say to anyone."

"You have no idea." Taz sighed as a fucking grin spread across his face. What was it about this son of a bitch? It was impossible to hate the fucker.

"Yeah, well, it's what we do." Steve looked back at the road. "We're one big dysfunctional clusterfuck of a family, but we have each other's backs."

Taz hadn't had a family of any kind for quite some time. He was starting to feel close to the Lee County guys, but family? He guessed since he was willing to risk his life for one of them, that's what they were. He had heard the stories of how the Warriors and the Lee County pack had joined forces. It seemed he was a part of that now.

"So, what's the plan?" Steve broke into his thoughts.

Good question. "Don't have one," Taz replied with ease.

He usually acted on instinct. Plans had a way of fucking everything up.

"Ah, so you're a pantser." Steve stopped at a red light, glancing at his phone and checking the mapquest.

Taz frowned. "What in the fuck are you talking about?"

Steve put his phone down and refocused on the traffic light. "Oh, sorry. Been doing some research. I'm thinking of writing my life story. Paranormal shit is big in the book world. Having a wife and baby, I need to make sure I have plenty of moola. Diapers ain't cheap, and believe me when I tell you little Drew Boo goes through a shit ton of them."

Having no idea where in the hell Steve was going with this story, Taz just sat back and waited. He had no choice anyway, because Steve didn't shut the fuck up. That was definitely one thing he had learned on this short drive.

"So, anyway, if you had a plan, you'd be a plotter as an author." The car behind them blew their horn. "Chill out, dickhead. Where's the damn fire, dipshit?" Steve yelled, glaring in his rearview mirror, then proceeded to inch his way under the now green light.

Taz was starting to hate Steve again. Once Steve was done fucking with the guy behind him, he continued with his "how to write a book" lesson. Taz really had no clue what the fuck he was talking about, but it didn't matter. Steve would continue in Steve fashion.

"Okay, where was I?" Steve had calmed down, looking at Taz as if he'd been hanging on to every word he had spoken. Taz had absolutely nothing to say. "Plan... plotter. Oh, yeah. So if you don't have a plan, you'd be a pantser. In the book world, that would mean you just wrote by the seat of your pants. Make shit up as you go and hope it all makes sense. That's me also. I'm a pantser. I don't plan shit, just go with the flow and hope to hell it works out."

"Where in the fuck do you come up with this shit?" Taz shook his head, trying to dislodge some of the bullshit spewing from Steve.

"Google." Steve snorted as if Taz was the biggest idiot he'd ever met. "Where else? Oh, and Siri. Siri knows a lot of shit. Even knows that ants have balls. Did you know that?"

Taz actually grabbed onto the door handle, ready to bail out of the hell he had found himself in until he heard Steve's next words.

"Okay, there's the house." Steve's voice became more serious than Taz had ever heard. "And looks like there's company. Hunter said if there was a car out front to stay away until it was gone."

They passed the house that sat pretty far off the main road. "Fuck that," Taz growled, his eyes narrowing. "Park."

"That's what I thought you'd say," Steve replied, then pulled into an empty lot. "You know, there are days I wish I was a plotter, 'cause I really don't know what the fuck we're doing."

Taz opened the van door with a sinister smile. "We're paying a friendly visit."

"Yeah, well, that smile on your face doesn't look too friendly." Steve got out, walked around and stood by Taz, who was glaring toward the house. "Lead the way, wolfman. This is your show. I'm just the backup."

Taz looked over at Steve and saw him in a totally different light. Before he could say anything, Steve pointed the key fob over his shoulder and pushed the button, locking the minivan with a goofy grin.

Jesus, this could get ugly.

∼

Leda stood like a deer in the headlights, unable to move. She knew her eyes and mouth were both wide open, but nothing came out.

"Hey, now." Malcolm walked up to her, wrapping his arm around her shoulder and pulling her close. "Don't come to my home talking to my girl like that."

"Your girl?" Minor frowned, looking Leda up and down, his eyes lingering on her breasts before going back to Malcolm. "Since when?"

"What are you, my dad?" Malcolm snorted, hugging Leda tighter.

"If she's his girl, why didn't you say something at the restaurant?" Minor walked farther into the house to where Jamie had sat straight up in the chair.

"Ah, maybe because she just met her," Malcolm answered for Jamie, then gave a dramatic sigh. "We met online."

"Online." Minor's face scrunched up as if trying to comprehend the word.

Leda realized Minor wasn't working with a full deck. She felt even sorrier for her friend who carried this dumbass's child.

"Yeah, man." Malcolm sounded irritated. "Online. Dating site. And why am I even explaining this? You aren't alpha, so it's none of your damn business."

That seemed to take the man's attention off Leda. "No, I'm not," Minor growled, his eyes narrowing at Malcolm. "But when Kingsman is gone, I'm in charge."

"Who the fuck says?" Malcolm sneered, pulling away from Leda as he took an aggressive step toward Minor.

"Ah, I'm Sandy." Leda tried to extinguish what was about to be a fight. She could feel it building and so could Jamie, who had slowly stood to move out of the way. "I didn't know she was Malcolm's sister. I was supposed to meet him at the restaurant, or at least that's what I thought. When he didn't show up there, I went to the address he gave me, here." God, she hoped this idiot bought it. If not, they were all in deep shit.

Minor gave her a quick dismissive glance before looking back at Malcolm. "You know how Kingsman is about newbies." Minor sniffed the air crudely. "At least she's one of us."

"I'll deal with the alpha," Malcolm replied, not budging an inch as he stared at Minor.

"Oh yeah, you will." Minor's laugh actually made Leda

feel physically ill. The asshole then turned to Jamie. "Come on and get home. I'm hungry."

"You just ate." Jamie sighed as she went to sit back down to put on her shoes, but Minor grabbed her arm roughly, stopping her.

"You back-talking me?" He sneered in her face.

"No!" Jamie's eyes widened in fear. "I, ah, just let me get my shoes back on."

Leda went toward them, but Malcolm stopped her by wrapping his arms around her and pulling her back against him. He gave her a warning squeeze. Watching her friend struggle to get her shoes on while the bastard just stood impatiently waiting without helping her had Leda screaming in rage on the inside. The bastard didn't even help her stand as she struggled to do so.

"It was nice meeting you." Jamie glanced her way quickly, then followed Minor toward the door.

Leda mumbled back, afraid to open her mouth too much. What she wanted to say would possibly get her and everyone else killed, so she bit her tongue and watched her friend walk out the door.

Minor stopped and looked back, first at Leda and then Malcolm.

"You have graveyard watch," Minor growled, his eyes dark with an evil she could feel. "Don't be late."

The door shut and the room became silent. They stood without moving, both just staring at the door. Finally,

Malcolm moved, but only his head so his mouth was against her ear.

"You have got to leave." His whispered words rang throughout her head, as did the images of Minor treating Jamie like trash.

Slowly, she shook her head. "Not until I finish what I came here to do."

CHAPTER 6

*T*hankfully there wasn't much traffic or people around. Taz really didn't think this was the main part of the town the pack resided in, because if that were the case, there would have been more people. Though this suited him just fine, it still made him nervous.

"Wait!" Steve stepped behind an old run-down structure.

Taz glanced to see a man and a pregnant woman exiting the house. He moved out of sight but had a visual of the man getting on a bike and the woman backing out in a beat-up truck. They headed down the old dirt road in the opposite direction, and as soon as they were out of sight, Taz took off in a run with Steve right behind him.

Missing nothing as he made his way up to the house and onto the porch, Taz went to knock, but his hand stopped.

Even in a short blonde wig, he knew the woman on the other side of the front door was Leda. His relief was short-lived as he noticed the man with his arms wrapped around her, his head lowered against her cheek.

"Ah, shit," Steve said behind him, clearly indicating he was seeing what Taz was seeing. "Calm down, man, and keep that wolf in chill mode until we know what's going—"

Taz reached for the handle, nearly ripping the knob off the door as he slammed it open. "Get your fucking hands off her."

"Okay, that was the other option I was hoping we could avoid, but guess not." Steve followed him inside with a long sigh.

"Steve?" The man frowned, looking up in surprise.

"Taz," Leda gasped, looking guilty as hell.

"Ah, I'm Steve." Steve held up his hand, then pointed at Taz, who ignored him since his eyes were zeroed in on the man touching Leda. "The one growling and foaming at the mouth is Taz. You must be Malcolm."

"I am." Malcolm nodded, his eyes going back to Steve. "I'm sure glad you guys are here."

"Yeah, well, if you don't remove your hands from Leda, you may be rethinking that." Steve nodded discreetly toward Taz. "Believe me, I know firsthand."

"What in the hell are you doing here?" Leda's eyes were still round with shock, then narrowed as they turned to look over her shoulder at Malcolm, who had finally let her go and stepped away. "Wait, what do you mean you're glad they're here? You contacted them?"

"Yeah, I did," Malcolm responded, not sounding sorry for that fact whatsoever. "Now they can get you the hell out of here before Allen gets back."

"I told you I would find you in my text." Taz's eyes glowed with anger, his body tense as his hands fisted at his sides. "That I know you read and refused to respond to."

"She does that when she's pissy," Steve added, then clamped his mouth shut when Leda turned her glare on him.

"And you." She pointed at him. "What in the hell are you doing here?"

"Oh, really, Leda?" Steve pointed back to her. "Why in the hell did you ghost me at my own wedding? Huh? I got questions of my own. Like where in the fuck did you get that wig?"

Her mouth opened, but nothing came out. She had missed his wedding. Damn.

Hatred for her uncle consumed her to the point she felt confused and claustrophobic. She had to get out of there.

Glancing from Steve to Taz, who just stared at her with such intensity that she felt it in her soul, she turned and headed toward the back door. Reaching the knob, she tried to open it, but it wouldn't budge. *Oh God! Please open!* She started to hyperventilate. The more she tried to jerk the door open, the more her breathing became restricted as tears of despair clogged her throat.

Feeling a presence behind her, she cringed, knowing it was Taz. His scent overwhelmed her. "Please, don't touch me," she whispered as her eyes closed. "If you touch me, I'll break."

Taz reached around her and opened the door with a mighty push, without touching her. She rushed outside, taking in deep breaths of air like a starving woman. She bent at the waist, hoping it would help her catch her breath. This was too much. Seeing Taz and Steve here sent her fears into overdrive. Now not only had she put Malcolm and Jamie in danger, but Taz and Steve. *Oh God!*

The strong hand on her back ran its way to her shoulder and squeezed gently. It felt right, was comforting, and even though she said not to touch her, Taz dared to do so only after giving her a minute. How could she want comfort so badly, yet her mind and heart screamed to push him away to keep him safe. She didn't know what to do. She should never have been put in this position, but her uncle had seen to it that she was no longer a child, but a woman who sought justice with a vengeance that no person her age should feel.

Slowly, she straightened, her eyes going to his. "You shouldn't have come," she whispered, the shaking of her voice prominent. "He will kill you."

Taz's hand left her shoulder and cupped her chin. "But he will never harm you."

"No." She shook her head. "You don't understand."

"Leda, I understand more than you realize, but this isn't the way." Taz searched her gaze. "Sam needs you. What happens to him if something happens to you? Then will he be the one seeking vengeance? Is that what you want?"

"I can beat him." Her voice grew stronger as hatred warmed her blood. "I've thought this through. I know what I'm doing. I'm doing this for Sam." Her chin trembled as a vision of her little brother floated through her mind. She sucked in her bottom lip and bit down, trying not to cry.

"My uncle will eventually find us. You don't know him," she finally choked out after getting her voice and emotions under control. "I have to stop him before that happens. You don't know him like I do, like this pack does. He killed his brother, my father. He won't blink before doing the same to Sam."

"Or you," Taz added, then sighed and pulled her into his arms. "I understand vengeance, *uwoduhi*."

His arms felt safe. *He* felt safe, and she soaked it in for as long as she could. Leda heard his words, then glanced up at him. "What does that mean?"

"*Uwoduhi* is Cherokee for beautiful." He didn't hesitate in his answer. "You should have come to me, Leda."

Her cheeks warmed from the blush shading them, but she frowned. "This isn't your fight."

"Yes." Taz's voice hardened slightly. "It is."

"Hey," Malcolm called from the door. "Hate to break this up, but you might not want to stand out in the open too long. It's not like I'm right in the middle of the pack, but anyone can be passing by." He indicated the woods not far from his house.

Leda pulled away from him and felt suddenly empty. She turned to walk toward the house, but Taz grabbed her hand, stopping her. "You are not alone in this, Leda."

Only giving him a nod and a small thankful smile, Leda headed toward the house, realizing she was squeezing his hand without letting go. Deep inside, she knew she was not going to be able to put him in danger any more than she could anyone else. She was alone in this. She had no choice despite wishing with all her heart it was different.

No one understood the evil she had witnessed at the hands of her uncle.

◠

Taz knew he hadn't broken through to Leda with the truth that she wasn't alone. He understood her anguish at not wanting to put anyone else in danger, but she would soon learn that he would not run. He was here and would be by her side, fight for her, die for her, but most importantly, love her and never leave her alone.

Walking into the house, Leda let go of his hand and walked straight toward Steve. Without a word, she wrapped her arms around him, giving him a hug. What surprised Taz was he didn't want to kill the bastard. When Steve gave him a look over the top of her head, Taz just gave him a nod. He knew Steve wasn't asking permission but was being respectful, which Taz appreciated.

"I'm sorry I missed your wedding." Leda's voice carried through the house, and everyone could hear that she was truly upset about the fact.

"It's going to take a lot of groveling for me to forgive you for that." Steve pulled away from her with a large frown. "It was the event of the year."

Leda sniffed and laughed. "I'm sure it was."

Taz hated to break up their little reunion, but his thoughts were not on weddings. No, they were on her safety. "How safe is she here?"

Malcolm gave him a long stare, then shrugged. "She's safer here than anywhere else in a ten-mile radius." Malcolm looked from Taz to Leda. "She'd be safer back with the Lee County wolves, that I know. You shouldn't have come here, Leda."

Watching her closely, Taz knew exactly what was running through her mind. She wasn't leaving, at least not without a fight. "What's the situation here?"

"Hell." Malcolm didn't hesitate in his answer. "It's pure hell. My sister is one of Allen's right-hand man's whores, and pregnant with his kid. Most of the females who came with Leda's uncle are treated the same way. Hell, what am I saying? Even their females are treated terribly."

"Did anyone get away?" Leda's eyes narrowed, but the hope in her voice rang true.

"Very few other than you and Sam," Malcolm responded, the sadness in his eyes evident to everyone in the room. "They have nowhere to go. Once Allen stepped in as alpha, no one dared challenge him because you'd have to go through all his men before even touching him. And once everyone saw...." Malcolm let his words fade off as he looked away from Leda.

Taz knew exactly what he was about to say.

"Saw what?" Leda asked, giving Malcolm only a second to answer. When he didn't, her face became red with anger. "Saw what, Malcolm?"

"Jesus," Malcolm whispered, squeezing his eyes shut. "I can't."

Taz didn't stop Leda from walking up to Malcolm. It was her right to know, yet Taz knew what Malcolm was holding back would change Leda forever.

"Malcolm, I'm going to find out one way or another. It's best coming from you." Leda's voice shook slightly. "Saw what?"

Even after Leda's words, Malcolm kept his eyes squeezed shut as if trying to block out the memories that had his skin pale. "I don't know how or when you and Sam escaped," he finally began but then stopped, his eyes opening. Everyone in the room could see the horror reflected in their depths. "Leda, I really don't think this is going to help you."

Taz watched Leda straighten her shoulders as if waiting for the blow Malcolm's words were going to deliver.

"Tell me, please." That time Leda's voice didn't shake but sounded stronger than Taz had ever heard it. Even though he was afraid of what was coming her way and how it could affect her, he was damn proud of the woman standing there with strength even he didn't know she possessed.

"They brought them out in front of the whole pack, alive," Malcolm hissed, his eyes narrowing, his face scrunching up as if in pain. "Allen demanded your father kneel before him."

"He refused," Leda whispered.

"Of course he refused," Malcolm said proudly of his previous alpha. "Then he brought your mom out, using her against him. She wouldn't let your father kneel."

Taz knew Malcolm was leaving a lot of the story out. Glancing at Leda, he knew she also knew that.

"What happened then?" Leda snarled, her hands fisted at her sides.

"You know what happened then, Leda." Malcolm sighed, wiping the sweat from his forehead. "Don't make me say it."

"No, I don't know because I ran." Leda's voice rose. "I ran away when they needed me most, Malcolm. I ran while you and others fought for your lives."

"There was no fight. We were too outnumbered and forced to stand and do nothing. It haunts me every single minute of every single fucking day. I hate myself for what I didn't do. And if you hadn't run, I would have had to watch you and Sam meet the same fate of the only two people other than you, Sam, and my sister that I called family."

"I deserve to know."

Taz watched a single tear slide slowly down her cheek, and he wanted nothing more than to hold her close and comfort her, but he didn't. Selfish as it may be, he knew if he wanted all of Leda, which he did, she would have to face this head on, and he needed to let her.

"Tell her." Taz took a step closer to Leda, and without touching her, he let the woman he loved know he was beside her. She was not alone.

CHAPTER 7

*L*eda fought with everything she had not to slam her hands over her ears. She didn't want to hear this but knew she had to. She had to know because that night haunted her every single time she closed her eyes. It haunted her every time her mind went silent.

To say she was surprised by Taz's words would be an understatement. She was sure he would be against her knowing whatever Malcolm was holding back. Slowly, she looked his way; his eyes were already on her. With confidence in her, he gave her a nod.

Taking a deep breath, she gazed back at Malcolm, ready for it all. "Tell me."

"Fuck," Malcolm hissed, then went to the fridge to grab a beer. He opened it, took a long drink, grabbed another one, then walked back to where he had been standing.

He didn't offer anyone else, but no one asked. "Jewel begged your father not to give in. No matter what, she pleaded with him not to kneel in front of that bastard. Jason had already been beaten so badly it took two men to hold him up, but once Allen threatened to have his men...."

Her breathing came in short gasps as if on the verge of hyperventilating again, but she controlled it best she could. "Malcolm, please."

"The fucker was going to let his men rape your mother in front of your dad and the pack, Leda," Malcolm spat out. "Jason tried so hard to get to Allen, but every single thing was against them both, and there was nothing we could do. We tried, but we were outnumbered. I swear we were."

Leda swallowed hard past the knot in her throat. "I know you did. I don't blame you."

"You can't blame yourself either." Malcolm eyed her, as if knowing that was exactly what she was doing. "Jason finally broke free and willingly fell to his knees, bowed before the son of a bitch to save Jewel."

"But Allen lied," Leda added as Malcolm paused to drink his other beer in almost one swallow. "Didn't he?"

"Of course he lied," Malcolm spat. "Oh, he played it to the max. He walked over and helped your mom to her feet, hugged her, giving her a kiss on the forehead." He stopped again, just staring at her.

She swore right then and there if Malcolm paused one more time, she was going to leap on him and strangle the words right from his throat. He must have gotten the hint, because his mouth opened once again and what came out of it seared her very soul.

"He slit her throat." Malcolm's voice choked with emotion. "I have never in my life heard such pain in a man's voice as I did in your dad's. It was as if her death gave him strength. He went for his brother, but Allen knew he was no match for Jason. Once your dad got the better of him, the other men Allen brought with him took your dad and beat him until Allen delivered the final blow."

"How?" Tears fell down her face, but she didn't move to wipe them away.

"Leda." Malcolm shook his head, unable to meet her gaze anymore.

"How?" she repeated without blinking, her tears still flowing.

"He decapitated him." Malcolm's voice was low, as if saying the words made them truer than they already were.

Finally, Leda blinked, her eyes closing and staying closed. Her shoulders shook slowly. Death by decapitation was the worst death for a shifter. Most believed that death in such a way meant they could not go into the beyond with their loved ones, which was the worst fate any shifter could face.

She felt Taz's hand on her back, but he didn't say a word. He just let her know he was there to comfort her, and at that moment, she needed it.

"Where is he?" Leda didn't open her eyes as she asked the question.

"He's gone and won't be back for at least two more days, maybe three," Malcolm replied after clearing his throat.

Her eyes opened, and she felt the hatred shining in their depths. And above all else, she knew the Leda from a few minutes ago didn't exist anymore. "I want to see the house."

"No!" Malcolm's voice became hard as he turned away from her, threw the beer bottles away and went for another.

Leda rushed toward him as he turned with another beer. "Yes, and I need you sober, so stop this shit."

"I haven't been sober since that night," Malcolm hissed, holding the beer out of her reach.

Punching him in the stomach, she grabbed the beer when he reflexively lowered his arm, and then she pushed him out of the way to stand in front of the refrigerator, blocking his path. "Tonight is a new beginning, then." Leda dared him to try her. She wasn't having it.

"Give it up, dude." Steve, who had been silent throughout the whole revelation, finally spoke up. "She's hardheaded."

Sadness erased the anger from Malcolm's face. "Just like her momma." He choked again. That time tears fell from his eyes.

Without thought, Leda grabbed him and held him

tightly. They had been friends since they were little, rarely apart as kids. It had always been her, Malcolm, and Jamie. She knew how much both of them loved and respected her parents. So many had. It was why she was there. Knowing her pack was being mistreated since their deaths told her that she had to do something, and by God, she would.

"I'm so sorry," Malcolm whispered in her hair. His tears dampened her skin. "I should have—"

"Shush." She held him tighter. "You should have done exactly what you did. Survive. I'm going to need help, Malcolm. You have to stop drinking, get it together. That son of a bitch is not going to get away with what he's done. As long as I breathe, he will pay dearly. A Kingsman does not go down without a fight."

He pulled away to look down at her. "Who are you?"

"Leda Kingsman," she said proudly, then wiped her face clean of tears. "And I'm here to get my pack and avenge my parents' death. I'm done running. I'm done hiding. You're either with me or not. Are you with me? It's a simple yes or no question."

Malcolm stared at her long and hard, then took the beer she didn't try to pull away and walked to the sink. Opening it, he poured it down the drain.

"Damn, you could have offered me that perfectly cold beer, ya know." Steve broke the silence in his usual Steve manner.

Leda nodded at Malcolm, then walked out of the kitchen past Taz and Steve, trying to find a room to have a moment to herself. Everything Malcolm told her was what she had feared happened. She wasn't naïve; she knew her parents had suffered at the hands of her uncle.

Slipping into a room, she closed the door quietly behind her, then walked toward the window across the room, looking out. But seeing nothing other than grief, she squeezed her eyes shut and tried to keep the scream of rage, loss, and despair from escaping her throat. It was too strong, the emotion fighting to break free. She covered her mouth with her hand, but it was no use. Her pain wasn't going to be held back.

Inside a strange room, her mouth opened, and what came out of it was every single pain her family endured. She folded into herself, giving her just a moment to grieve before the hatred overtook her.

Taz's eyes never left Leda as she disappeared down the dark hallway. He couldn't even comprehend the pain she must be feeling. Knowing he had to give her a minute to herself, he forced himself to stand still. If he moved, it would be toward her.

"Why in the fuck did she make me tell her?" Malcolm sank down on the old beat-up couch, laying his head back with his arm over his eyes.

"It was her right to know," Taz answered, finally pulling his gaze away from where she disappeared.

"You know," Steve said thoughtfully, as he walked closer

to the two men, "at the moment, these assholes are outnumbered."

"Uh, there're three of us, man." Malcolm kept his eyes covered. "Allen left twenty of his men behind to keep us all in order. Twenty-one if you include me."

"You work for the bastard?" Taz's eyes narrowed, suddenly on alert.

That time Malcolm moved his arm away from his eyes to stare at Taz. "Fuck you, man," he hissed. "I know what you're thinking and fuck you. I have no loyalty to the fucker. This is me surviving and keeping my sister as safe as I can."

"He didn't mean anything by it," Steve jumped in. "He's a little overprotective with Leda." Taz and Malcolm stared at each other for a few more seconds before Steve cursed. "For shit's sake, who's here for Leda? Raise your fucking hand." Steve's hand shot up as he looked between the two men.

"I am, but I'm not raising my hand," Malcolm replied, daring Taz to contradict him.

"Okay, that's two, and I know grump-ass over there is. So how about we shut the fuck up and listen to Steve, hmmm?" Steve lowered his hand as he paced around the room. "Here's my thinking. If we gather all who want to leave the pack, do it while the alpha shithead is gone, would they go?"

"Some would." Malcolm sat up, listening intently to Steve. "Actually, most would, but a few holes in that plan. One, we don't have the manpower, and two, they aren't going anywhere that there won't be protection. Obviously, none in this pack is alpha enough to over-throw Allen, so once they found us, we'd be back to where this all started and in worse shape."

"I'm pretty much a badass, but you're right. We don't have the manpower at the moment, but within a few hours, we will. Between my guys and the Lee County wolves, we can make the twenty motherfuckers left here playing God cry like little bitches. Keep one alive as a warning gift to the piece-of-shit so-called alpha."

Taz liked the plan. Go figure. "Go on."

"Actually, that's it." Steve frowned. "I can't come up with every damn thing."

Malcolm stood with a new fire in his eyes. "If we have nowhere safe to go, I'm not going to chance putting all these good people at risk. They've been through enough. Allen will be out for blood if we pull this off, and once he found us, he'd make us pay dearly."

"*If* we pulled this off." Steve snorted. "Oh, we *will* pull this off, no doubt about that. What do you think, Taz?"

"Believe it or not, I agree," Taz replied, happy Steve had stopped calling him Tax. "But the quicker we do this, the better. Once the alpha is back, some may be too afraid to move."

Before anyone could say another word, a scream of pain echoed down the hallway toward them. Taz felt it in his soul, and his wolf howled in his mind as he raced toward the sound. Opening the door, he walked in to see Leda bent at the waist holding onto herself, her body shaking with the weight of grief. He walked over and took her in his arms, allowing that pain to transfer to him.

"Let it go, Leda." Taz held her tightly, and as her body shook against his, he swore that the bastard who tore her life apart would pay with his own. His eyes flared as his expression turned to stone while the most precious gift he had ever been given fell apart in his arms. "I've got you, *usti ayastigi*," he whispered against her head, then repeated it to himself, *I've got you, little warrior.*

CHAPTER 8

*L*eda felt spent as she held onto Taz as if he were her lifeline, and at that moment, he really was. She'd lost it but knew her body and mind had needed to let go. Since the day she'd run with Sam, she'd kept everything bottled up, having her little brother to think about. He was her responsibility, and still was to this day. As long as Allen Kingsman walked this earth, her brother was not safe. That was going to change.

"Thank you," she whispered against Taz's chest.

"Never thank me." Taz led her to the bed and eased her down, sitting next to her. "Not for taking care of you."

Leda wiped her face free of tears. Her eyes felt swollen, as did her face. "Why are you being so nice to me?" Leda frowned, thinking she knew the answer but wanting to hear it from him. There was guilt in her question. "I haven't always been nice to you."

A rare smile formed on his lips as he clipped her chin gently with his hand, angling her face closer to his. "No, you haven't." His response was soft and teasing. "But you aren't very good at being mean."

After everything she had just learned, she couldn't believe how at ease she felt with him and how easily his words, even in jest, had her smiling. "Guess I'm not." Her smile slipped slightly. "I'm sorry, Taz. You just confuse me."

"I do that to a lot of people," he agreed with a thoughtful tilt to his head. "So all is forgiven."

"Why are you here?" Her smile was completely gone now as she moved away from his touch. "If it's to stop me, then it was a wasted trip."

"I'm here because I belong by your side." Taz wasn't smiling either. Before she could say anything at all to deny his words, he added, "Tell me you have no feelings for me."

"And if I do—" She bit her lip before continuing. "—you'll leave?"

"No, because I know you'd lie to me and everyone out there, saying you hate us just to keep us safe. That's not going to work," Taz replied knowingly. "But if you tell me now that you have no feelings for me, as soon as this is over, I will disappear, and you won't have to deal with me again."

His words hit her hard and deep. Even the thought of never seeing him again after this ended, whatever *this* was, tore a hole through her heart.

"Say the words, Leda," Taz urged, his eyes searching hers, looking for the truth. "Tell me you have no feelings for me. It's that easy."

Slowly, Leda shook her head. "No, it's not that easy." Reaching out, she took his larger hand in hers as one last tear fell. "Because without really knowing you, I can't even imagine my life without you in it."

Taz leaned down, his lips inches from hers. "You will never have to imagine, because I will always be by your side, no matter what."

Their lips met, and in that instant, Leda knew she belonged to this man. There was no more doubt or denying that fact. It frightened her, but she accepted it. As their kiss deepened, she also realized that before she could give her whole heart to Taz, she needed to close this chapter of her life, and it was only fair to let him know.

Reluctantly, she pulled away, then reached up, touching her lips. "Before I can promise you anything, I have to get my life back," she whispered, hoping he understood. "It wouldn't be fair to you if I didn't tell you."

"Leda, my *usti ayastigi*, I would wait for eternity for you." Taz leaned down, sealing his words with a kiss.

"What does that mean?" Leda loved when he spoke in his native tongue.

"Little warrior." He smiled, brushing the hair from her wig away from her eyes. "And as soon as we leave here, we will burn this thing."

A laugh spilled free. "I agree 100 percent. It itches so bad." Leda reached up and adjusted the dreadful thing. "So have you and Steve made nice?"

Taz frowned with a shrug. "As long as he is happily mated, I think I can tolerate him."

"He's a good guy, Taz," Leda replied with a grin. "Who knows, maybe you can become the best of friends."

"That may be pushing it." Taz shook his head. "Do you have feelings for him?"

Leda thought long and hard on that question. The more time she took, the more emotion she saw cloud Taz's eyes. "No, I don't." She reached up and slowly touched his jawline, reveling in the fact that she was able to caress him, something she'd spent hours imagining. "I'm even wondering if I ever really did, other than friendship."

Taz placed his hand on top of hers. "Then he'll live."

She didn't know how serious he was being, so she remained silent. At least they weren't trying to kill each other, yet. "That's good to know." She dropped her hand.

"Well, at least I'll promise he can live for now, because honestly, the asshole has come up with a pretty solid plan that I think you need to hear." Taz stood and held out his hand to her.

Anxiety filled her. "Okay, I'm ready." She stood, taking a deep breath as her hand met his. "I think."

"You are ready, Leda." Taz led her out of the room. "It's time you take your life and pack back."

Leda stopped him before they left the darkened hallway. His words meant so much to her that it physically hurt, but a good hurt. "Thank you."

"For what?" Taz frowned down at her, confused.

"For understanding and not trying to stop me." Leda squeezed his hand. He didn't say anything for a long moment as they stared at each other.

"I do understand, but also know I won't let you put yourself in danger." His voice hardened slightly. "We will figure the best way about this, but you fighting the alpha for the pack is not going to happen."

Disappointment settled in her gut, but she also understood him. He was a man, an alpha male in his own right, and for her to think he would be on board with her doing something like that wasn't reality. But she also knew if it came down to it, then that was exactly what she would do. Either way, Allen Kingsman would die by her hand, one way or another.

Knowing she couldn't lie to him, she just gave him a short nod before proceeding out of the hallway. His slowness clued her in that he wasn't reading her nod the way she had planned, but he remained silent.

Malcolm and Steve sat at the kitchen table talking. Both turned to look at them, focusing on Taz first, then her.

"I hear you have a master plan." Leda cleared her throat as she looked at Steve.

"I always have a master plan." Steve puffed out his chest, then frowned. "Usually no one wants to hear my master plans, but this is a good one."

Leda offered him a small smile as they walked to the table. Taz sat down and pulled her onto his lap. She didn't fight the move. Her wolf was restless, as was the woman, and his closeness eased them both. It was a good feeling, one she hadn't experienced in such a long time. "Okay, let's hear it."

As Steve relayed the plan of bringing in the Warriors as well as the Lee County wolves, Leda's agitation grew. It sounded great, but her mind kept going back to the mates of these men who would be putting their lives on the line, and for people they didn't know.

"I don't know." Leda couldn't look any of them in the eye. "This isn't their fight, and if someone got hurt or killed, I couldn't live with that. It's already killing me that you three, as well as Jamie, are involved."

Leaning toward her, Steve frowned. "Do we look like pussies to you?"

"Ah, no," Leda hedged, not knowing where Steve was going with this. "But—"

"Hell, Leda." Steve rolled his eyes. "Buts are two ass cheeks with a line down the middle. There are no buts to it."

"Okay, that made no sense." Malcolm eyed Steve as if he'd lost his mind. "Let me."

"Makes perfect sense to me," Steve shot back, then

waved toward Leda as if telling Malcolm to go right ahead. "No one ever understands *the* Steve," he mumbled, then discreetly winked at Leda, but Taz saw it and growled.

"At first, I was against it, but—" Malcolm gave Steve a warning glare and looked back at Leda. "—it makes the most sense. This is what the Warriors do. And maybe the Lee County wolves will take us in. With them, we could be strong and—"

"No!" Leda shot off Taz's lap. She began shaking her head.

"Way to go, man," Steve said out of the side of his mouth to Malcolm. "Should have let me continue with my 'but' analysis."

Malcolm stood and faced down Leda. "That is our only hope."

"We have to find another way." Leda continued to shake her head.

"There is no other way." Malcolm's desperation became louder, making Taz stand up.

"There is another way. The way I planned since I ran out of those tunnels. The plan I came here to do." Leda's voice topped Malcolm's. "I should never have come here. I should have stayed hidden until I took him out."

"And you'd be dead or made an example of by now," Malcolm shot back with a hiss. "Did you not hear what they did to your parents? Allen has more hatred for you than anyone I know." Malcolm's eyes widened at what he'd confessed out loud.

"What?" Leda tilted her head, catching his slip. "I thought he gave up looking. That's why I waited so long."

"Your uncle hasn't given up shit where you or Sam is concerned." Malcolm's laugh was bitter. "Anyone who can claim alpha status at the age of sixteen could petition the elders if they have proof that your uncle in fact killed the alpha of the Kingsman pack, your parents. In turn, Sam could be granted the pack back and Allen sentenced to a life as a renegade."

Leda gasped as she started to remember her brother's teachings. His were always more interesting than hers, so she'd always listened in. "So when my brother turns sixteen, he could go to the elders with proof of what happened?" The highest elders belonged to no pack in order to be fair during such judgments and disputes. Their final word was law, and anyone who went against their final word was banished from any pack or allowed to form their own. No one wanted their business to go to the highest elders.

"Factually, yes." Malcolm nodded, his face grim. "In reality, no."

Taz had stood beside Leda during the exchange. "Because your uncle will make sure he doesn't reach that age." Taz took a step between Leda and Malcolm. "But he's too young to have a bounty on his head."

"But she's not." Malcolm looked toward Leda and then away.

Before she knew what was happening, she was pushed toward Steve as Taz went for Malcolm straight across the table. Malcolm was no match for his speed or strength. In a blink of an eye, Taz had him pinned to the floor with a wicked blade against his throat.

"She has a bounty on her head?" Taz growled.

Leda pulled away from Steve so she could see Malcolm's face as he answered.

"Yes," he wheezed, not even fighting as the knife pressed harder against his throat.

"Taz, stop." Leda put her hand on his shoulder. "Why didn't you tell me?" A knot of gut-wrenching betrayal formed in her stomach.

"Because I needed the money to get my sister out of here," Malcolm said as tears rolled from his eyes. "But I changed my mind, Leda. You're my family. I can't—"

"Shut up!" Taz pushed harder on the knife; a streak of thin red blood curved down toward the floor. "How much?"

"He just raised it," Malcolm said, then swallowed carefully. "To… fifty thousand."

"Oh my God." Leda's legs wobbled, but Steve was there to keep her upright.

"I swear, Leda," Malcolm cried out, his eyes wide with fear. "I couldn't do—"

"Slit his fucking throat," Steve growled beside her.

"Any last words, motherfucker?" Taz hissed as he readied himself to do what Steve ordered.

"Oh God!" Malcolm tried to fight one last time, but Taz

was too strong. "Please, my sister didn't know anything. I swear. Please help her, but don't hurt her. Leda, please."

Leda stared at her childhood friend with such remorse it almost brought her to her knees. This was all her uncle's doing. "You searched for me with them, didn't you?"

"Only once, I swear it," Malcolm cried. "Only once, and I came home alone to drink myself to death because of the fear that I might have actually been the one to find you."

"Would you have turned me over?" Leda knew her voice was cracking, but she didn't care. There was no hiding her devastation.

Malcolm squeezed his eyes shut. "I honestly don't know." He didn't reopen his eyes. "I swear to God, I hope I wouldn't have, just like I changed my mind to turn you over when Minor came in the door. I swear, Leda, I just couldn't do it."

"I don't believe him," Steve said as he glared down at Malcolm.

"Then why would I have tried to contact someone to get her?" Malcolm pleaded his case. "I could have just turned her over, collected the money and been done with it."

"Ehh, still pretty fucking shady." Steve acted like he was weighing his options of what to say next. "Fuck it. I say send the bastard to Hell. Just thinking of doing something like that is a piece-of-shit loser move."

"No." Leda leaned down to reach for the knife, but Taz used his shoulder to nudge her away. "Let him go, Taz."

"Oh my God." Jamie's voice caused them all to look up, except her brother who was seconds from death. "Malcolm!"

CHAPTER 9

az's rage was close to being out of control. To think Leda had been alone with this asshole before he and Steve arrived sent fear and anxiety throughout his body and mind. Just another inch and he could easily make sure this bastard was never a threat to Leda ever again. What stopped him from doing just that? Her. Leda's voice had the power to stop his hand from making that fatal move.

Hearing an unfamiliar voice had Taz looking that way, but he still controlled the bastard underneath him. A pregnant woman stood just inside the door, staring at him in horror.

"Let him go," Leda urged him. "Please."

Looking back down at the man, Taz sneered as he pressed the knife even harder at one side while he lifted it slightly on the other, just so the man knew how close to death he had come. "If you even think about causing her harm, I will hunt you and kill you slowly, with so much pain and suffering you can't even imagine it in your worst nightmares."

"I swear it," Malcolm promised as another tear slipped from his eyes. "I never wanted to hurt Leda. She's my family."

"She is nothing to you," Taz warned as he released the knife from the man's throat.

Malcolm's hand went instantly to his neck as Taz stood, making sure his body was between this bastard and Leda. He didn't trust him, not even an inch. He hoped to hell releasing him wasn't something he was going to regret later.

"You won't." Malcolm stared at Taz. "You won't regret this," Malcolm swore, as if he could read Taz's mind.

Before Taz could warn him again, the pregnant woman ran to Malcolm's side. "What's going on, Leda?" she asked, looking at Taz. "Who are you, and why did you have a knife to my brother's throat?"

"Your brother planned on turning Leda in for a bounty." Steve didn't hesitate to answer with true disgust in his voice. "And you're damn lucky he's breathing right now. I wanted his head."

"Malcolm?" Jamie stepped away from her brother in horror. "Please tell me that's not true."

Leda went to step forward, but Taz stopped her. "Did you know there was a bounty?" she asked.

Jamie shook her head, but her words contradicted the action. "We've heard rumors. If you don't work for the alpha, you're not privileged with information. We've never known what happened to you or little Sam. Every day I've prayed you made it, and then to see you in the restaurant…. Why did you come back?" She turned toward her brother without waiting for an answer and slapped him hard across the face. "You lied to me. I asked you if the rumors were true. You told me they weren't. You knew she and Sam were still alive."

Malcolm didn't even rub the red handprint on his face. He just moved to head for the fridge.

"I swear, if you go for a beer, I will shove it up your ass," Jamie bellowed, her eyes blazing fire. "Why, Malcolm? Why would you do something like this, and to Leda? My God, to Sam. He idolized you."

Taz watched Malcolm stop; his shoulders turned inward at each word his sister spoke as if he were deflating. His head hung low with his back turned toward them all. "Because I can't stand to see you with Minor. It was the only way I could think to get you away from him, Jamie."

"You had no right to put that on yourself. Dammit, Malcolm! How could you do this?" Jamie's eyes filled with tears and her hands went to her face. "I'm so sorry, Leda."

Stepping around him, Leda took the woman in her arms. "It's okay." Her voice was calm, and Taz was impressed with her compassion. He was still reeling at the thought of how close she had come to being…. He couldn't even think about it. His eyes flared back to Malcolm, wanting to kill him all over again.

"You really don't know what it's been like here since that night." Jamie held onto Leda, her face buried against her neck. "It's inhumane, the way they treat us."

Taz watched Leda's shoulders stiffen at the woman's words. She was taking this personally, which was dangerous.

"We do have a plan," Steve added, then sighed. "But your bro kinda mucked that up."

Taz watched the woman's eyes light up. He wasn't sure if he even trusted this woman. No, he didn't. He trusted no one when it came to Leda. Only himself.

He glanced at Steve and shook his head, warning him to keep quiet. Steve nodded but continued talking. *Jesus.*

"Honestly, not sure how much we can say, because fifty grand is a lot of money." Steve frowned, crossing his arms. "Some would even say enough to turn in your own kid."

"Can it get us out of here? Away from this place?" Jamie's voice cracked with emotion as she stared first at Steve, then Taz and finally back to Leda. "Please, I'll do anything to get away."

"Even turn over the woman you just hugged?" Taz put out there, just to see her reaction.

Jamie sneered his way, her eyes narrowing. "Never." She then glanced at Malcolm, who had finally turned around to face them, but his eyes were downcast. "I'm loyal to the true Kingsman alpha, and that was Leda's father. A man who took us in without question and treated us like his own."

Jamie's gaze met Taz's, and he believed the truth she spoke, to a point.

"I swear on my baby's first breath," she sealed her promise.

To swear on your unborn child was unheard of. "Jamie," Leda whispered, her eyes watering. "You don't have to—"

"Obviously I do since my name is associated with his." Jamie glared at her brother. "I will do anything you need me to do to make this happen."

"Jamie, you can't," Malcolm finally said. "If Minor finds out, he'll kill you."

"Fuck Minor," Jamie spat, earning a large smile from Steve.

"I like her." Steve nodded, then glanced toward Malcolm. "You, not so much."

Taz frowned, realizing they needed to trust someone for this plan to work, and other than having Leda fight her uncle, which no way in hell was that happening, this was their only option. "I'll call Dell."

"I've already called Sloan, and they're ready to go." Steve held up his phone. "One text and he'll coordinate with your peeps."

"What's the plan?" Jamie asked, but no one answered her, clearly indicating the trust wasn't there 100 percent.

~

Leda watched Taz walk away but stay close enough, no doubt so his eyes were on Malcolm, who was staring at her. She really didn't know what to say to him; her heart hurt terribly. He had been so close to betraying her, and she didn't know if she could ever forgive or trust him.

Taz walked back over, his face a mask of fierce hardness. "I just talked to Dell over the speaker with Garrett, Marcus, and Hunter. They're getting everyone together now."

"Oh damn." Steve rubbed his hands together. "There's going to be some major ass kicking going down in this place tonight."

"And they all agreed that the ones who have been loyal to her father are welcome into the pack as long as they pledge their loyalty to Dell, until her brother is old enough to make a decision to take over his rightful place," Taz announced, his eyes on Leda.

Jamie's gasp turned into sobs of happiness. "Is this really happening?"

"Sounds like it," Steve replied, then glanced at Malcolm. "Guess you better be getting your shit straight, man. I've got a friend who can read you like a book, and believe me when I tell you I'll be using him to find out exactly what the fuck you're about."

"I need to talk to Dell." Leda didn't feel as excited as everyone else. "This is going to bring Allen to Lee County. I'm not only putting Sam in danger but everyone else by doing this."

"He knows the risks, Leda," Taz reassured her. "But when he gets here, you can talk to him. Okay?"

Leda nodded as other worries plagued her. "How are they all going to come in without being seen?"

Jamie snorted bitterly. "Minor and the rest of the assholes are probably drunk by now." She rolled her eyes. "How do you think I'm here? When the alpha is away, little boys play. They think they're unbeatable and never have watchers as they should. Right, Malcolm?"

"Yeah." Malcolm's voice sounded gravelly. "It's true. They're unbeatable."

"No one is unbeatable." Taz's eyes narrowed.

"How are we going to decide who comes and who's loyal?" Leda asked, not wanting to walk anyone into Lee County who didn't belong.

"Oh, we have our ways." Steve winked at her, then frowned when Taz growled at him again. "Man, chill the hell out. It's just a wink."

"Keep it open when looking at her unless you want to start wearing a patch... permanently," Taz warned, wrapping his arm around Leda.

"I don't feel good about this, Taz," Leda confided, not knowing who else to trust. "This is going to lead him straight to Sam."

"No one is going to lay a finger on Sam," Taz promised her. "I swear it. And no one is going to harm you either."

"But this is my fight," she whispered, still not sure about the plan and how fast this was all taken out of her control. Maybe she didn't have the full grasp of what she was doing, but she had a plan. This was far from it. Yet Taz's promise of safety for her and her brother warmed her heart like nothing ever had.

"Not anymore," he whispered, holding her tighter, though she still didn't feel at peace. A large knot of doom lodged in her heart, and she was afraid it was going to explode. Everything she had ever held dear could come to an end. Her eyes met Taz's, and she prayed this time that wouldn't be the case.

CHAPTER 10

Taz knew Leda was torn. The hours they sat waiting for the Warriors and the wolves to show were eating away at her. He could see her indecision growing. Finally, she was talking with Jamie and seemed to have relaxed. He watched her closely, loving the way she became expressive with her hands as she got excited with a story she was telling.

"You should let me—"

Both Taz and Steve said no at the same time, not letting Malcolm finish whatever he was about to say.

"You aren't doing shit until my buddy gets here." Steve was texting on his phone, not even looking at Malcolm. "Until then, shut it."

Someone knocked on the back door, sending Steve and Taz into action. Taz looked toward Jamie. "Open it, but stay clear, just in case it's not our guys."

Jamie nodded as Taz motioned Leda toward him. Once she was within reach, he stashed her behind him as Steve got into place. Jamie opened the door slowly, keeping her body positioned away from Taz and Steve.

"Jamie?" an unrecognizable man's voice asked. He saw Steve relax and knew this was one of the Warriors.

"Sloan," Steve said, then rushed over to open the door more. Fourteen vampire Warriors walked into the house, each sizing everyone up.

"Dell isn't here yet?" the man who Taz knew was the leader of the Warriors asked as he glanced toward Taz.

"No, they had a little farther to travel than you," Taz replied as he held out his hand. "I'm Taz. Thanks for coming."

Sloan gave him a nod and a firm handshake. Introductions were made all around, and then there was Malcolm.

"Adam," Steve called out. "I need your expertise, my man."

Taz watched a younger guy walk toward Steve. He had heard of the different powers some of the Warriors possessed and was curious to see exactly what this guy named Adam could tell them.

"This is Malcolm," Steve said as all the Warriors gathered around, staring at the man. "He was once a good family friend to Leda."

"I still am." Malcolm frowned, his eyes narrowing.

"That remains to be seen," Steve growled, glancing

toward Jamie, then back to Malcolm. "Leda showed up here without knowing there's a bounty on her head by her uncle. This guy remained quiet about the fact. Though he didn't turn her over when he easily could have, there are some trust issues."

There was another knock on the door. Everyone became deadly still, staring at it. "Wolves or unwanted company?" Damon asked, his voice as deadly as his eyes.

"No one uses the back door, so it has to be the wolves," Jamie replied and went to answer it. Slade stopped her and Taz knew he was the doctor. He'd been to Lee County several times with his mate, Jill, who stood beside him. She took Jamie's arm, gently moving her out of the line of danger.

"Allow me." Slade waited until the women were safely away before nodding to Jared to open the door.

"Well hell, you're still ugly," Jared said as he stepped out of the way so Hunter could walk in.

"And you're still not funny." Hunter snorted as they shook hands. "That your minivan we parked next to across the road?"

"Fuck no!" Jared snorted, then glanced at Steve. "I'll give you one guess who's driving that."

"Why all the hate on my minivan? It's multifunctional." Steve frowned with a hiss. "Damn, can't a man drive a family car without getting shit for it?"

"No!" many voices rang out.

Dell was the last to enter the room, his eyes immediately

going to Taz and then Leda. His frown deepened. "We have a lot to catch up on," Dell said as everyone looked past Taz to Leda. He wanted to push her farther behind him but knew it was their alpha's right to reprimand her. He just hoped Dell didn't go too far with it, because no way in hell did he want to tango with that big son of a bitch.

"You're all just in time." Steve saved Leda from more of a Dell-lashing, drawing everyone's attention toward him. He explained again what Malcolm had almost done. There were a few growls coming from the large group, which barely fit in the house.

"How much is the bounty?" This was from Garrett, who had yet to say a word to Leda. Taz wondered about that as well.

"Fifty thousand," Steve answered, then glared at Malcolm.

Every eye went to Leda, and a few whistled at the amount. "He got that money to pay out, or is this just a bullshit amount?" Marcus asked.

"No, he has it," Malcolm replied, his eyes going past Taz to Leda. "He's had all control over the finances from Leda's parents."

"And you think he would actually pay it?" Duncan's eyes narrowed in disbelief.

"For her, he would." Malcolm glanced at Leda, then away quickly. "No doubt about it."

"Damn, girl." Hunter glanced at her. "You better be nice to me. That's a nice chunk of change."

"Exactly. So you see, we have trust issues here. Malcolm says he's had a change of heart, but that's a lot of cha-ching, and I don't fully believe him." Steve glanced at Adam. "Will you do the honors of letting us know if he lives or if he's going to die by Taz over there? Inquiring minds want to know."

"Malcolm, you be truthful," Jamie warned her brother with a frown.

"Oh, it doesn't matter. Adam can read anyone," Jill said beside her. "He won't be able to hide anything from him."

Everyone watched as Adam laid his hand on Malcolm's shoulder. The frown on his face grew harsh as he stared down at the man. Finally, he let go. "He isn't going to do anything to her... now." Adam gave Malcolm one last hard stare. "But it did cross his mind more than once. He did it for his sister, to get her away from the man who's keeping her against her will. The money would have helped them get away."

"I'm the sister, and not once did I ask him to do anything like that." She held her arm up to Adam. "Go ahead. I don't want anyone here thinking I would turn her over for money. I would rather rot here than do that. Go ahead. I want everyone to know."

Adam touched her wrist gently and smiled. "Truth," Adam confirmed, then glanced at Malcolm. "But you have a hell of a road ahead of you with your sister."

"Damn straight he does." Jamie crossed her arms, resting them on her big belly.

"Okay, we're here." Sid glanced around at everyone. "Whose ass are we kicking, and how many? I'm good for five."

Taz grinned, liking all the Warriors immediately. They were his kind of people for sure.

Leda wasn't as happy as Taz. She walked around him, looking at everyone. "There are people here who are still loyal to our father but are afraid." She glanced at Jamie, then at Garrett, who just glared at her. "I don't want them hurt."

"This could be complicated." Sloan frowned, looking at Garrett and then Dell. "How do you think we should go about this."

"Leda is well loved by our pack," Jamie said and walked toward Leda. "If they knew she was here, they would follow her anywhere."

"No." Taz shook his head. "She's staying here."

"Ah, no," Leda said quickly, heat behind her words. She knew Taz was trying to protect her, but he still failed to understand that she felt she didn't have a choice but to stand strong and be involved every step of the way. "She isn't."

"Listen," Jamie jumped in, no doubt before things got out of hand. "Especially with the alpha gone, these boneheads go up to the main house and party most of the night. They are so full of confidence that no one will dare come onto their land that no one is watching anything." Jamie looked at all of the new faces. "Not one of you were stopped, right? You all got in undetected and with ease no doubt?" Several nods of acknowledgment that she was accurate appeared from both the Warriors and the wolves of Lee County. "Once Allen is back, it will tighten up some, but in a few hours, these guys will be toast."

Everyone looked at Adam. "Truth."

"Wait a minute." Jamie frowned. "He wasn't touching me."

"Most of the time I don't have to." Adam shrugged. "If I felt I needed to, I would."

"Fair enough." Jamie shrugged back.

Leda walked over to where Garrett stood quietly. "How's Sam?"

Garrett looked down at her, and at first, she didn't think he was going to answer. "He misses you." His tone was matter-of-fact. "He's worried. His stuttering is worse."

"It always is when he's nervous." Leda felt like her insides were being twisted. "I'm sorry, Garrett. I didn't mean to bring this to your door."

Garrett sighed, his features softening somewhat. "You really think I'm worried about that, Leda?"

"You should be," she responded without hesitation. "I didn't want everyone involved. It's why I lied and left. I didn't want all of this."

Garrett narrowed his eyes at her. "Well, you got it." His response wasn't said with meanness or blame. "You're part of the Lee County pack. This is what we do. I knew your father. He was a good man and didn't deserve what happened to him. It's our right as packs to defend those who cannot defend themselves."

"You knew my father?" Leda gasped in surprise.

"I hadn't seen him in a long time, but yes, I knew him and your mother, Jewel." Garrett reached out and pulled her into his arms. "I'm sorry for your loss. It was a big loss, and you and Sam didn't deserve this. Taz told us what happened and I'm damn sorry, Leda."

"Thank you." Leda sniffed, holding onto Garrett. She had never had anyone to depend on after her father and mother died. It had only been her and Sam until she'd met Janna. "And I'm sorry."

"Don't be… this time." Garrett gave her a fatherly squeeze. "But next time you do anything like this, I will ground you forever."

Smiling, Leda nodded. "After what I've been through this past week, I'd welcome being grounded to my room."

"Oh really." Garrett chuckled as he pulled her away to look down at her. "So I'm not going to get the 'I'm too old to be grounded' routine?"

Suddenly feeling exhausted and older than her years, she slowly shook her head. "Not today."

CHAPTER 11

Taz looked up when Sid spoke. "It's go time, boys and girls." Sid glanced at his watch. "Everyone know what they're doing?"

"If not, wing it," Jax said, heading for the door.

Devon walked over to Taz, giving him his hand. "Sorry I've given you a lot of shit, man."

Taz stared at him for a long minute, wondering what the fuck was going on. First Steve, now Devon.

He grasped Devon's hand, their grips tightening for a firm shake. "No worries." Taz still didn't like Devon, but if they were going to have each other's backs in times like these, they needed to at least respect each other.

Devon glanced toward Leda, who stood alone, looking lost. "She sure has been through some shit." Devon sighed. "Takes a pretty strong person to get through what she's been through. You're a lucky man."

"I am," Taz agreed with pride. Knowing Devon realized he had no chance with Leda made him like the asshole just a little bit more.

"Wait!" Jamie called out before everyone filed out the back door. "Malcolm, Leda, and I need to lead the way. Those who are still loyal to Leda's father will see you all as a threat at first. Give us time to explain along the way. Word will spread fast, maybe even to the main house before we can even get there."

"Yeah, I don't think so." Taz didn't like that idea at all. Leda being out in the open without protection was not happening.

"Listen, Minor thinks she's a girl Malcolm met on the internet. She still has her wig on, so if you guys scatter while we gather up whoever we can, this can work." Jamie put her hand on her waist with a frown. "I'm telling you, if we all go marching through town, it's going to get ugly, fast."

"We do ugly really well," Sid announced, gaining agreement from most of the group.

"And you really think that hideous wig is going to work?" Hunter tugged at it, gaining a smack from Leda.

"It already has," Jamie replied, then glanced around at all of them. "Most of Allen's guys have only seen a picture of Leda, but the ones who watched her grow up are going to know her with the wig. Guys, we have elderly people who can't fight. We need time to get them to safety."

Dell stepped up and looked around at everyone, then back to Jamie. "Where is the main house?"

"At the end of town," Leda answered instead of Jamie. "It's a large three-story with white pillars along the wraparound porch. You can't miss it."

"Can five of your guys surround the house without being seen?" Dell asked Sloan, gaining snorts from the Warriors.

"'Can we surround the house without being seen?' he asks." Jared cranked his neck back and forth. "I think we can handle it."

"I can call for some of my friends." Katrina grinned, standing next to Blaze.

"Keep them for later." Sloan nodded toward her.

"I don't like not knowing the layout," Marcus stated. "And how sure are we that most of his men are at the main house?"

"Oh, that's easy." Jamie grinned proudly, then glanced behind her at the clock on the wall. "I'd say the stripper I ordered should be showing up just about now. They'll be there."

"That's a guarantee that if some of them aren't there, they will be soon," Malcolm added knowingly.

"I say we shut the fuck up and go take care of business." Damon frowned with impatience. "We could stand here all night saying what can go wrong."

"He's right," Blaze replied, speaking up for the first time. "We know what to do, so I say let's get it done."

"I think Jamie and Leda need to stay here," Steve added, then stepped back when Leda glared at him with a growl.

"Think again," Leda snarled with narrowed eyes.

Taz actually liked that idea a lot. "We can keep a few of us here so when the ones who want to leave head toward the cars, the small group here can direct them."

"Won't work." Jamie shook her head. "You guys think you know what you're walking into, but you don't. These people have been treated like garbage. They've been lied to, stolen from, beaten, threatened and some killed in front of the others as a lesson. You seriously think any of them will go on a word of a stranger? They'll think it's another game Allen and his assholes like to pull when they're bored. Test their loyalty. Honestly, if that's the way this is going to go down, then I'm out of here, and I suggest you all leave us as we are, because you will definitely make it much worse, especially for me if it's discovered that I helped you in any way."

The room became quiet as they digested her words. Taz glanced at Leda, whose anger clearly showed on her face at hearing what her pack had been through.

Shit, there was no way she was going to stay back now.

Leda watched as plans were made and everyone took off

at different times. She knew what her job was, and she'd be damned if anyone tried to stop her from doing it. This was not what she'd expected when she'd come here, but if she could help some escape from her pack, then she'd do it.

"I won't let you out of my sight." Taz touched her cheek as he stared into her eyes. "You need me and I'm there."

"I know." She nodded, then glanced back at Malcolm, who had been very quiet. "You think I can trust him?"

"Trust no one but me," Taz warned, then smiled at her wide-eyed expression. "Sorry, I'm a little possessive."

"A little?" She raised her brow, then kissed his cheek. "I'll be careful. The quicker we do this, the better for the pack."

"We can't have Malcolm stay behind, because even with Adam reading him, he's still not trusted." Taz glanced his way. "Plus, we already had another talk, and I think he has an understanding of what will happen to him if he goes against us."

"Oh, I'm sure that was some talk." Leda chuckled, which was the last thing she wanted to do, but she was staying positive that this was going to work.

"You ready?" Jamie walked up to Leda and gave her a hug. "Thank you for coming back."

"It's been my plan since the day I left," Leda assured her, giving her a squeeze. "I'm just sorry it took me so long."

Leda started following Jamie, but Taz stopped her as

Steve and Malcolm passed them. "Watch yourself, and remember my eyes will be on you the whole time."

"I know." Leda nodded, then went on tiptoes to kiss him. "I trust you, Taz."

Something crossed his face that she couldn't quite read, but then it was gone. "Go on." Taz put his hand on the small of her back as she caught up with Malcolm and Jamie at the car. Getting in, she turned to look, but Taz nor Steve was anywhere in sight.

Leda sat in the back while Jamie drove and Malcolm sat in the passenger seat. "You think this is going to work?"

"I know this is going to work," Jamie replied, backing out. She put the car in gear, heading toward their small shifter town that Leda was anxious to see again. It was only about a mile and a half to the edge of their small town.

Everything was so familiar, yet different. Run-down and deserted, the sight gave her a chill as she realized the last time she was there, her mom and dad had been alive, only to be murdered shortly after her departure.

Leaning forward, Leda looked out the front windshield, her stomach flipping over at the sight of her home at the end of the main street. Every light in the house was on, and she could hear the music playing from inside the car that far away. Anger raged through her body as she glared at the house.

"It's changed," Malcolm said as he turned to look at her over the seat. Their eyes met for a brief second before he turned back around, and she saw the remorse in their depths. "Everything has changed."

Jamie parked far down the road from the main house. "Come on, we're going door-to-door." She turned the engine off, then turned around to look at Leda. "You ready?"

With a nod, Leda got out of the car, glancing toward her house. Yes, she considered it her house still, because no one gave her uncle the right to have it. He had not only stolen her parents from her, but her house, and it was time she took it back. "I'm more than ready."

As they walked toward the first house, Leda realized who lived there, or who had lived there—Mr. and Mrs. Watkins, an older shifter couple who ran the old sawmill. As they made their way up to the front door, she saw the curtains move in the large window. Even though the lights were out, she knew someone was there.

Jamie and Malcolm went up together with Leda following. Before Jamie could knock, the door cracked open. "Mr. Watkins, it's Jamie. Can we come in?"

"I don't want any trouble." Mr. Watkins's voice shook as he peeked out, trying to see Leda.

"We're not here to cause you any trouble," Malcolm said, glancing behind him at Leda. "There's someone we want you to see."

"Malcolm, my Beth isn't feeling very well," Mr. Watkins said as he tried to close the door, but Malcolm put his foot against it to prevent it from closing. "Please, we don't want any trouble with the alpha."

Leda gently moved Jamie aside as she walked up onto the porch. "Mr. Watkins, unfortunately the real alpha of Kingsman cannot cause you any problems, nor, if he were alive, would he." Leda pulled the wig off her head, letting her long brown-streaked hair flow around her. "As his daughter, I'm here to try to help you and Mrs. Watkins, along with the others who have remained loyal to Jason Kingsman, my father."

CHAPTER 12

*A*s soon as Leda disappeared into the house, Taz ran toward the back of it. While the door opened to reveal an older man, that wasn't the problem. She was alone inside with Malcolm, and he didn't trust that son of a bitch.

Seeing a back door, he and Steve went for it and was surprised when Malcolm opened the door for them. "Told you I could be trusted."

"Yeah, that's still up in the air, bud." Steve walked past him as Taz pushed past them both. He walked in to see Leda with an older woman in her arms.

"Oh, child," the woman cried. "We thought for sure you and little Sam were dead."

"Please, Mrs. Watkins," Leda urged the older woman. "Calm down before you upset yourself. You don't want to make yourself sick."

"Who are you?" Mr. Watkins asked, his voice full of distrust.

Leda looked away from Mrs. Watkins to see Taz standing in the doorway staring at her. "It's okay." Leda smiled, reassuring him. "He's a friend."

Taz cocked his eyebrow at that but smiled at the older man. "We're here to help."

The man reached out his hand. "Thank you." His voice trembled with emotion.

"We have to get to the others," Jamie started to explain. "Take just what's important to you. Hopefully sometime soon we can come back to get the rest of your belongings, but for now, just small things that you can't do without."

"Oh my." Mrs. Watkins frowned. "I don't think I can leave my things. It's all we have."

Taz and Leda shared a look, but Leda jumped in. "I promise you that when we can, we will return for your things. What's important is to get you out of here, if that's what you want."

"It is." Mrs. Watkins nodded as tears leaked from her aging eyes.

"We'll get more things, Beth." Mr. Watkins nodded at Taz, letting him know he would take care of his wife. "Where are we going?"

"Steve is going to take you to someone." Taz ushered them toward the back door. "Trust them. They won't let anything happen to you. You'll be safe."

"Bless you." Mrs. Watkins placed a cold wrinkled hand on his cheek. "You're a good boy."

Taz had been called a lot of things, but that wasn't one of them, and yet the woman's words softened his heart. He would make damn sure these people got the hell out of here safely.

And so it went, house to house. Each person or family was shocked to see Leda alive. Most cried, but all were ready to get the hell out of there.

As Taz followed in the shadows, only to go in once Malcolm opened a door, he noticed how run-down everything seemed. It was as if the pack had given up, and the more he saw, the more people he met, he knew that was what had happened. But the hope in their battle-weary eyes when they saw Leda and heard about Sam told him how respected her family had been by this pack. Taz finally understood more what was driving Leda to do something as crazy as walk into this place and fight for her people. These were definitely her people, and it showed with every new face he saw.

Soon, they arrived at the last house. Word had spread, and people were ready to leave out their back doors. Steve couldn't handle it all, so Katrina and Jill started to help escort people to where all the cars were parked.

As soon as the last were out of the house, Taz watched Leda walk to the window and open the curtain just enough to look out. He knew she was staring at her home. It had grown louder the closer they got. No one was really going in and out. A few staggered around on the porch, but they wouldn't have been aware of any of them in the shadows.

Alcohol didn't affect shifters the same as humans. They had to drink a lot for it to affect them, but the effects didn't last long. He wanted Leda to go with Katrina and Jill as they took the last of the ones leaving, but he knew it wasn't even worth saying. As if reading his thoughts, she turned toward him.

"I have to do this my way." Leda looked at him with determination and a hint of pleading in the depths of her beautiful eyes. "I have to. If I don't, then none of this will have been worth it."

"Can you tell me what you have planned?" Taz asked hesitantly before agreeing to anything. He knew what their plan was, but he had a feeling Leda's was totally different.

"No." She shook her head, then rushed toward the door and was out before he could move.

Jamie jumped in his way, and he had to stop himself from barreling her over.

"Dammit!" He picked Jamie up, gently moving her aside, and ran out of the house.

Leda raced toward the house as she bent to scoop something. He bolted toward her. When she was right in front of the house, she reared back her arm and let loose a rock, shattering the glass in the front door.

His blood went cold.

~

As soon as the rock left her hand, she let out an inhuman roar. "Get out of my fucking house!"

The music went silent as the front door slammed open. "Who in the fuck broke my window?"

Minor stepped out onto the front porch, his eyes finally landing on her.

"I did," Leda yelled, the anger in her voice unmistakable. "It's not your window. It's *my* fucking window."

That seemed to shut him up, but only for a second. "Listen, girl." Minor tossed his beer bottle in the weeds off the porch as he came to the top step, his eyes running her up and down. "Unless you want to come in and join the party, you best run along. And we'll talk about how you're going to pay for my window tomorrow."

He turned to walk back into the house, but Leda bent down, grabbed another rock and hit him in the back with it.

"I said it's not your window," she growled. Anger like she had never felt before punched her square in the chest, making her body vibrate with rage. "It's the alpha's window, and that sure as hell isn't you. You're too stupid to be alpha."

Other men had come out of the house, as well as a half-naked woman, but Leda didn't care.

"Listen, you stupid bitch." Minor took a step off the porch, but before he could go to the next step, every single Warrior and Lee County wolf came out of the shadows. Taz walked beside Leda, with Jamie and

Malcolm on the other side. "Jamie, what in the fuck are you doing?"

"Minor, she's right. You are such a dumbass," Jamie sneered at him. "And as to what I'm doing, I'm leaving your ass."

"Not with my kid, you're not." Minor rushed toward her, but Devon clotheslined him before he got anywhere near her. The rest of Allen's thugs became restless, but the growls from the other side kept them at bay.

"Go anywhere near her and I'll kill you." Devon stood over Minor in a deadly pose. "Got it?"

Minor army-crawled backward until he was far enough away from Devon to get back on his feet. His eyes shot toward Leda, studying her hard before they widened. "I'll be damned."

"Yes, you will be," Leda replied, then looked around what used to be her home. "Did any of you have a part in killing my mother and father?"

Gasps and whispers could be heard as everyone started to realize exactly who she was.

"Did you?" she bellowed, taking a step forward with Taz right alongside her. Actually, everyone on her side did the same. She was well protected.

After the shock wore off his face, Minor glared at her. "We've been looking for you, sweetheart." He looked her up and down slowly. "The picture didn't do you justice."

Leda felt Taz stiffen and start to make a move forward, but she reached out, blocking him. Not that he couldn't break free whenever he wanted. "Where's my uncle?" she hissed, ignoring his remarks.

"Boys, you know who we got here?" Minor smiled, rubbing his hands together.

"I see a bunch of pissed-off VC Warriors," one guy in the back said.

"And that dude"—he pointed toward Hunter—"was the shifter on television who outed us."

"Sucks to be famous." Hunter shook his head, but the grin on his face was sinister. "Hey, dumbasses, you're both right. Pissed-off VC Warriors and Lee County wolves about ready to rip through you. So how about coming on down here to save us the trip of coming after your sorry asses?"

Minor held his hand up as if his men were making the first move. None of them were. "I'm not talking about them, you stupid fuckers. I'm talking about her." Minor pointed at Leda. "Ms. Fifty Thousand Bounty just landed on our doorstep. Leda Kingsman is in our house."

"*My* house, asshole," Leda growled, noticing the change in all the men on the porch. No longer did they look around at the others with fear. No, now they were looking at her as if she were one big dollar sign.

"Get her the fuck out of here!" Taz hissed toward Steve, who stood behind her.

"No." Leda frowned as the men on the porch started to separate slowly. "This is my fight."

She screamed as Steve picked her up and took off running. He was going too fast for her to see anything except Taz looking away from her as the men on the porch tried to give chase.

CHAPTER 13

*T*az had known this was a fucking bad idea. Now Leda had an even bigger target on her head. "Fuck!" he growled and went for the first mother-fucker who tried to pass him to get to her. He knew Steve would protect her with his life; it was why he'd called for the vamp to take Leda. She was going to be pissed, but he'd deal with that later.

Jumping, Taz tackled the asshole trying to pass him, then rolled up to his feet, as did his opponent. The guy glanced to where Leda disappeared and back to him, then attacked.

Taz was more than ready. Once he started getting the better of the guy, the asshole began to shake. Before the bastard could shift, Taz jumped in the air, spun and kicked the guy in the throat. He went down like a brick.

Taking in the scene, he noticed the Warriors were

holding their own, even with the ones who'd shifted. He glanced toward where Leda had gone and saw figures disappearing into the darkness. Knowing things were being handled, Taz took off.

Not one of those bastards would lay a hand on her.

Turning, he ran between houses, hoping to cut them off. As soon as he rounded the corner, something struck him in the head, sending him to the ground, dazed.

"Going somewhere?" a rough voice hissed.

Shaking his head to try to get his bearings, Taz moved only his eyes, his gaze landing on the man's feet. With everything he had, he lifted his body with his arms, twisting himself, and swept the man's feet out from under him with his legs. As soon as the guy landed on his back, he rolled. Taz was ready. He pounced on top of the guy, raining blow after blow to the man's face with his fist and elbows. All he could think about was getting to Leda, and this bastard was in his way. For a split second, Taz lost focus as he glanced to where he knew Steve took Leda.

His arm was grabbed, and Taz was rolled to where he was on the bottom, and the man let loose with his own blows. Protecting himself the best he could, Taz took the hits, waiting for his opening. It wasn't long before the asshole grew tired, allowing Taz to swiftly trap both his arms and rise up as he pulled the bastard down and headbutted him. Then he used his body weight to flip the piece of crap over his head.

In one rapid movement, Taz jumped to his feet, turned, and stomped on the guy's face. A sickening thud echoed in the darkness. Without even checking the guy, he took off.

Four men were heading toward the old building where all the cars were parked and everyone waited. Dammit, he wasn't going to make it.

Fear like he'd never felt before coursed through his body. If anything happened to Leda, it would be his fault. He couldn't even imagine her being hurt. He'd seen the pack's greed when they'd learned who she was. They weren't after anyone who stood behind that building other than her, and he'd sent her away from him, where he couldn't protect her.

His legs and arms pumped hard and fast. They were almost there. Suddenly, a lone figure stepped out from behind the building. He squinted, trying to see through the darkness with the bright light shining behind the person who was definitely female. *God, please don't let it be her. Don't let it be Leda.*

Just before the men reached her, a strong wind blew against him from his back; a strange chirping sound rang out around him as a black swarm went straight over his head toward the men and lone woman.

Knowing he was going to have to shift to make it in time, Taz stopped himself as the swarm of black dropped in front of the woman, blocking her and the light. "What the…?" Taz slowed and looked on in awe as thousands of bats swarmed the four men. They backpedaled toward him.

"Holy shit!" one man yelled as he stumbled backward. Bats swooped down toward them. Suddenly they parted as the woman, who Taz realized was Katrina, Blaze's mate, walked through.

"I suggest you turn around and go back." The woman's voice was strong and sure. "You don't want any of this."

Something caught Taz's attention out of the corner of his eye. He glanced that way to see six huge coyotes stalking toward the men from the sides. They hadn't seen them yet.

"Just give us the girl," one man ordered. He swatted at one of the bats that dove toward his head. "Then we'll leave."

One of the coyotes raised its head and howled loudly, causing the men to look that way and shift their position, only to find out they were flanked on both sides by the creatures.

One of the men looked toward Katrina. "What the hell are you?"

"One badass bitch with an attitude," Katrina replied, then snapped her head up to the sky as bats began to dive-bomb the men, sending them running his way.

Taz was more than ready to intercept.

They didn't even see Taz until they were upon him, too focused on running away and swatting the bats as well as keeping a distance from the coyotes on their ass. Taz reared back and punched the closest one, sending him to the ground knocked out cold.

He looked at the other three.

"It's either them or me." Taz gave them a sinister grin as

he cracked his neck back and forth, stepping into a ready stance. "And I hope to fuck it's me."

The three rushed him, but the coyotes cut off two of them, growling and nipping, keeping them at bay. Damn, that was one hell of a power Katrina had.

"Come on." The man waved Taz on. "You ain't shit."

Taz punched out, hitting the man square in the nose, which burst like a balloon full of blood. The man's head bobbed before he punched out, but Taz easily dodged it. That time, Taz doubled up, hitting the man in the nose again and sending an uppercut right under the chin. The guy stumbled back a few steps.

"You need help, man?" Taz heard Steve shout.

Laughing loudly, Taz shook his head. "Nah, man." Taz kicked after dodging a few more pitiful punches his way, sending the guy on his ass. One of the coyotes nipped at the man, sending him to his feet.

"But you ain't shit," Steve taunted. "Come on, dude. I'm missing all the fun. At least you can let me have one of them."

Taz spin-kicked the guy in the jaw, knocking him out on his feet until he crumbled to the ground. He glanced over at the other guys, and two of the coyotes backed off, leaving the man free for Taz.

The guy looked down at his friend on the ground, then back at Taz and took off. He didn't get far before the coyotes took him down.

"Get up, you pussy." Steve reached down, grabbing the guy up, and began to pound on him.

"And that leaves one." Taz's head snapped toward the last one who just stood, staring at him in fear. "What? Not a badass since I'm not an innocent woman with a bounty on her head?"

"I, ah...." The guy stammered all over the place.

In two steps, Taz punched the guy with everything he had, dropping him where he stood. He didn't have time for these assholes. He needed to make sure Leda was away from here and safe.

He continued to walk toward the woman who once again looked to the sky. A moment later, the bats disappeared as fast as they came. The coyotes also turned and trotted off toward the woods.

"Pretty amazing power." Taz gave her a nod of respect as he passed her. "Thank you."

"You're very welcome." She smiled and turned to follow him as Steve ran their way.

"Hey, at least I got my hands on one of those assholes." Steve cracked his knuckles and snorted. "Even though he was a big pussy."

As soon as they turned the corner, Taz's heart froze for a beat. "Where's Leda?"

Leda's body shook with anger as she stood with everyone. She cursed Steve up and down, but he didn't care.

He just glared at her as she continued to curse him. Katrina and Jill were with the frightened shifters waiting to escape this place, and now so was she. She needed to be down there. She was done running. This was her pack. This was her—

"What's that sound?" she asked Jill, who stared at where Katrina had just disappeared.

"Stay here," Steve said as he followed Katrina.

"What is that?" she asked Jill again.

That time, Jill glanced her way and smiled. "Come here."

Leda followed her and stopped when she saw four men running toward Katrina. A breeze had kicked up, blowing her hair back as the sound of a weird clicking grew louder. "Are those bats?"

"They sure are." Jill nodded toward Katrina. "She can communicate with animals. Isn't that freaking cool?"

Leda watched as the bats swarmed above Katrina's head and just as the men reached her, they dropped, forming a wall, separating them. Within a few seconds, there was a split where Katrina walked through, with Steve following.

The crowd behind them became restless, so Jill turned to calm them down, leaving Leda watching in awe. Then it dawned on her. She wasn't being watched. Glancing back at Jill to see her talking to the group, Leda backed away and disappeared into the darkness of the building. If she crossed the road, she could bypass all of this and head back toward the house where she belonged.

It wasn't long before she was running past the now empty houses. The fighting was still going on, but it was obvious her side was winning. She stepped over bodies, not even knowing if they were alive or dead. She knew it wasn't any of their people, and that was all that mattered.

Glancing quickly around, she didn't see Taz, but she did see Dell and Garrett head into the house. Crossing the yard, she jumped up onto the porch and stopped just outside the door, staring in.

Memories slammed into her even though the inside looked nothing like she remembered. There were pieces of her past left, but not much, and it broke her heart. What had she expected? She felt stupid for even hoping, but that was all she had left. Hope. Now looking around, her hope was crushed.

Slowly, she stepped inside and took a deep breath, but the smell was far from her home. She passed the stairs, only glancing that way before heading toward the kitchen. Hearing Dell and Garrett, she backtracked, then went up the steps.

Her eyes searched each mark on the wall, every piece of dirt on the floor as she made her way upstairs. Once at the top, she stopped and turned. At the end of the hallway was her parents' room. She headed that way but stopped in front of her door, which was cracked down the middle. Quickly, she reached for the knob and opened the door, letting it bounce against the wall. Nothing of hers remained. Nothing. She went to the next door and opened it. Sam's room was the same, empty of his belongings. Once again, she turned, passed the bathroom door and finally stopped in front of her mom and dad's room.

Rage, fear, sorrow as well as emptiness consumed her as she opened the door. Her gasp of shock echoed in her ears. The room was unchanged. She stepped inside, her hand over her mouth as she stared in awe and horror. Everything looked the same. The bedspread, curtains and even the top of their dresser contained the same things that were there on the day their lives were taken. Glancing toward the walk-in closet, she frowned. Slowly, she stepped that way and opened the door. Their clothes still hung inside.

Moving inside, she touched one of her mother's dresses, then lifted it to her nose to smell. Her scent still hung to the fabric. Her heart hurt as she reached for one of her dad's shirts and did the same. She buried her face against it, breathing in deeply as sobs escaped her throat.

Suddenly, a sense of awareness stunned her, as if she were afraid to be caught in her mom and dad's closet, almost as if none of the past had happened. The feeling was strange.

Backing out, she screamed as a hand shot out of the clothes, grabbing her arm in a bruising grip.

CHAPTER 14

*T*az scanned for any sign of Leda, but so far nothing. He swore right then and there he would never take his eyes off her again, even though he knew that was impossible. The fighting at the house was over. He jumped over bodies, then skidded to a stop.

"Have you seen Leda?" Taz asked the closest person to him.

"No." Jared frowned as he nudged a body with his boot. "I thought she was with Steve."

"Fuck!" Taz was going to lose his fucking mind if he didn't find her. Trying to calm himself, he closed his eyes and began calling to his wolf.

"Jesus, Damon." Sid's voice brought him out of his trance as he opened his eyes to see Sid staring down at a head. "You really need help."

"Sorry," Damon said, but didn't sound sorry at all. "Sometimes I just can't help myself, and the mother-fucker grabbed my nuts."

"Ah," Sid hissed as if just the words pained him. "Then yeah, definitely off with his head."

"You find her?" Steve rushed up as he looked around. "Damn, Damon, again?"

"Grabbed his nuts, man," Sid replied as he continued checking for life.

"Ouch." Steve grabbed his junk with a cringe on his face. "Definitely the wrong nuts to grab."

"Why in the fuck weren't you watching her?" Taz grabbed Steve by the shirt. "I trusted you to keep her safe."

"Whoa." Jared jumped between them. "We'll find her, but you need to chill the fuck out."

Taz glared at Steve for a second longer before turning away to backtrack. He had taken two steps when he heard a scream coming from the house. It was Leda.

He took off immediately, pushing past anyone in his way. Just as he ran through the door, he heard noises coming from upstairs. Garrett and Dell along with Hunter were coming from the other side of the house at a run.

Taking the stairs three at a time, Taz landed at the top, then turned to see Leda being pulled back into the last room at the end of the hall. She was fighting like crazy to get away.

"Hey!" he bellowed as he started that way.

Leda appeared with a man behind her, his arm around her throat, using her as a shield.

"I swear I'll snap her neck." The guy's voice was high-pitched with fear.

"She won't be worth anything to you dead, asshole." Taz figured he might as well try to use the bounty to get her away from the bastard.

"I don't care about the fucking money." He stared wide-eyed over her head. "I saw what they did to them out the window. The big fucking vampire took Denny's head off. Jesus, who the fuck are you guys?"

"You let her go and you can walk out of here," Taz lied. He saw the blood at the corner of Leda's mouth. That and that alone called for this man's painful death, and he would be the grim fucking reaper.

"Yeah, I don't think so." The guy tightened his grip, making Leda gasp and gag. "You need to move out of my fucking way and give me a clear path. Once I'm free, I'll let her go."

No way in hell was that happening. He looked at Leda, then shifted his eyes to the right. He did that twice before looking back at the man, who was no doubt still trying to figure out how to escape with his head intact. Holding his hand out, Taz moved his body to the side so the man couldn't see his other hand as it reached toward the waistband of his jeans.

"Listen, man, I just want her," Taz said calmly. "Let her

go, and you have my word you can walk out of here. What do you say?" His fingers touched cool steel.

"Fuck you and your word," he spat. "I swear I'll snap her fucking neck like a stick if you don't—"

In one swift and seamless movement, Taz pulled the knife and hit his target dead on, right in the forehead. "Wrong answer," he growled, racing toward Leda before the man could take her down, but he wasn't close enough. She fell backward from the man's dead weight, going down.

Reaching her, Taz pulled the bastard's arm from around her neck, then pulled her up. "Are you hurt?"

She rubbed her throat, shaking her head. "No, I'm fine," she croaked with a grimace. He didn't believe her as he continued to check her body, but she started to push him away. "I'm fine, dammit."

The fear and anger at seeing her with that bastard's arm wrapped around her neck flooded him all at once. "What in the hell were you thinking?" His voice rose with each word.

He heard footsteps running up behind him and turned to growl, his teeth showing. Seeing it was Garrett, Dell, and Hunter, he relaxed, then turned back to Leda. "Answer me," he hissed, lifting her face to meet his.

Slowly, her eyes rose to meet his; they were haunted with an edge of distrust... of him.

What the fuck?

≈

Pushing fully away from Taz and his touch, Leda stood on her own two feet. "I had to see." She cleared her throat, which felt tight. She didn't know if it was because of the man's arm that had been squeezing it or the tears she was holding back. God, she was so damn sick of crying.

Taz glanced around, his frown deepening. "You put your life in danger just to see this room?"

For a split second, she wanted to smack him for not understanding. "You had Steve take me away." The accusation was clear to everyone within hearing distance.

"Yes, I did." Taz seemed fine with his decision.

"You had no right to do that," Leda growled, taking a step closer to him.

Taz remained silent, but the anger on his face and rage behind his eyes said more than words could. Actually, she noticed everyone was looking at her, some angry, others disappointed.

"I shouldn't have run off like I did. It was wrong, but until you've been in my shoes, do not judge me or my actions. None of you would have let me come here because of the danger, and I understand why, so give me the benefit of understanding why I did it. I may be younger than all of you, but I'm not stupid and honestly, what I've seen and been through has aged me well past my years. But I had to see this place one last time before I left. This was my home, a good place before my uncle took it away. It was my right to walk through the halls and rooms to know what I've started here today was the right decision." Leda stared at each of them before looking back into her parents' room. "And now that I have, I know my decision to leave Lee County to fight for my pack was most definitely the right one, and no one had the right to take that away from me."

Hunter started to say something, but Leda held up her hand, stopping him.

"I never wanted anyone else involved. My fear of getting anyone else hurt or killed was always at the forefront of my plans, which totally changed because of everyone here now. But I thank you for standing with me, Sam and my pack. I know it doesn't seem like I give a shit as I rushed toward the house, but I also think I'm afraid to ask because of what the answer may be." Leda swallowed hard, then looked toward the ground as her stomach soured at the fear of what her next question may bring. "Was anyone hurt?"

"Ah, well...," Hunter hesitated. "There were a few injuries and, ah, deaths."

"Our side?" Her heart clenched painfully.

"Fuck no." Hunter's head shot back as if he couldn't even believe she'd asked that. "Not a scratch."

"Good." Relief spread through her. "Please don't move the bodies. Leave them where they lie." She looked at Dell when she said it, keeping her gaze from Taz, who was glaring holes through her.

Turning, she walked farther into the room and went to her mother's dressing table. Reaching down, she grabbed a picture of herself and stared down into it. The girl in the picture didn't exist anymore, and it was time, way past time that Leda let that girl go.

Holding the picture to her chest, she glanced around the room.

"My room and Sam's no longer exist. Nothing of ours remains." She spoke with such control she surprised herself. "But this is… *was* my parents' room, and it looks the same as it did the day they were murdered."

"That's strange." Garrett walked into the room, looking around, then swiped a finger over a piece of furniture and examined it. "Someone's been keeping it clean."

"I didn't tell you everything." Malcolm's voice had her turning his way. He stood behind Taz, staring into the room. "I'm sorry."

"I think you need to start talking." Hunter's voice became hard. "She deserves to know everything. Plus, if you don't, I think Taz may kill you on the spot."

Leda glanced over to see Taz restraining himself from going after Malcolm. Garrett had actually put himself between them.

"What else can there be?" Leda sighed, walking toward Malcolm. Seeing the stark paleness that colored his face, she knew the answer to that question. A lot, there was still a lot she didn't know, and she was terrified to hear more.

"Do you seriously think that Sam's age has anything to do with Allen not putting a bounty on his head?" Malcolm asked, as if wanting her to guess what he had to say.

"It's against—"

Malcolm snorted. "Come on, Leda. Think!" Malcolm took a step forward, but stopped when Taz growled low in his throat. "You think your uncle is such an upstanding citizen that he wouldn't do it? Sam is more of a threat to him than you could ever be, or so everyone thinks."

She was getting sick and tired of trying to guess what in the hell her uncle could do, or already did. Hell, she was sick to death of Allen Kingsman. "Dammit, Malcolm, just tell me!" Leda rushed toward him and smacked him on the chest. "What haven't you told me!"

Malcolm didn't even try to protect himself. He just stared down at Leda until finally his gaze shifted away as if he couldn't stand looking her in the eyes. "Sam isn't...." He swallowed hard. "Sam is Allen's son."

Stumbling back as those words sank in, Leda shook her head and laughed. "No." She stared at Malcolm as if he'd lost his mind. Her laughter died as he finally looked down at her. The truth in his eyes hit her like a brick. "No!"

"Allen blackmailed your mom." Malcolm frowned, ignoring Leda shaking her head. "He was in love with Jewel and wanted everything your dad had. He promised her that he would leave if she spent one night with him. If she didn't, he would stay, fight your father, and take everything he had, even her if she didn't. She did."

Leda smacked him across the face. "You're a liar!" she

spat, then went to slap him again, but stopped when he didn't even try to defend himself.

"I wish I was, Leda." He his eyes went to the ground. "Right before my mom died, she told me everything. Jewel had confided in her. They were like sisters. You know that."

She did know that. *Oh God. This can't be true. It can't.* Bile rose from her stomach, burning its way to the back of her throat. "My mom would never do something like that. She loved my father."

"Leda, you don't even know the evilness that your uncle possesses," Malcolm continued, his voice becoming harsh. "Everything he threatened your mother with happened. Look around. You've seen what he's capable of. That's why she did what she did. She loved your father, her family so much that she sacrificed herself to the bastard, but in the end, it was her downfall."

Still holding the picture, Leda gripped her stomach, trying to keep from vomiting. The more Malcolm talked, the more she knew he was telling her the truth.

Her eyes rose from the floor to Malcolm, just as Taz wrapped his arm around her. She let him. "He left," she whispered. "I remember him leaving. It was maybe a month later Mom said she was pregnant with Sam."

Malcolm nodded. "My mom told me that because your dad was alpha, news of her pregnancy didn't leave the pack."

Leda knew that to be true; it had been the same when Janna was pregnant. It was considered that alphas became weaker, more vulnerable when their mates were pregnant.

"He showed back up years later and put two and two together after seeing Sam," Malcolm added. He continued, as if knowing what she was about to say, "I know for a fact Sam is Allen's son."

"How?" Leda was afraid to ask, praying that maybe, just maybe, this was a mistake. That somehow it wasn't true.

Malcolm glanced first at Taz, then back to Leda. "The night my mom took her last breath, she told me that Jewel confided in her. About Sam. About everything."

"I don't understand." Leda frowned, without a doubt knowing she was about to be sick. "Why would your mom tell you any of this?"

There was such a long hesitation that Leda thought she was going to have to rush out of the room before Malcolm answered, but he finally did, and God, she wished he hadn't.

"Because she knew I loved you." Malcolm swallowed hard, then lifted his head to stare down at her. "She made me promise to keep you, Jewel, and Sam safe and, on her last breath, I did. I swore it. I've failed you all. I'm so sorry."

Malcolm walked past her, his hand moving behind her mother's dresser. He stilled as the sound of ripping tape echoed in the room. When his arm and hand reappeared, he held a small journal. Walking over, he handed it to her.

Leda put the picture under her arm and took the journal,

running her hand over it and wiping off the dust. Opening it up, she saw her mother's beautiful hand-writing.

"Everything is in there," Malcolm whispered, his voice choked with emotion. "All of it. No one knows. I thought that night… ah, Allen would tell everyone, but he didn't, and as far as I know, he hasn't still. But—"

"But what?" Leda urged him to finish, even though she didn't know how much more she could take.

"Just before your father was… killed, Allen whispered something to him. I have never heard such a sound of anguish come from a living bei—"

"That's enough!" Taz cut him off, and he was right. It was enough.

Slapping the journal shut, Leda pushed past everyone. Hearing Taz calling out to her, she ran into the bath-room, slamming the door behind her. The picture fell from under her arm onto the tile floor, the glass frame smashing into pieces. She barely had time to lift the toilet seat before her stomach emptied into the bowl. The one thing she didn't drop was the journal; she held onto it tightly as she continued to heave all of her emotions out of her body.

CHAPTER 15

*T*az barged into the bathroom just as Leda fell to her knees. Knocking broken glass away from her with his foot, he reached down, catching her hair with one hand while gently holding her forehead. "I'm here, Leda," he whispered, then cursed when he saw blood on the toilet.

He glanced at the picture she had been holding; it lay face up, showing a beautiful, carefree Leda with a cheesy grin on her face. Her hair was blown back in a summer breeze as she tilted her head, looking into the camera. His heart beat frantically as he held the same girl's head as she heaved at what she'd learned about her family. If it took his last breath, he would make things right for this... not girl, but woman.

"Oh God," she whispered as she started to sit back. He sat beside her and pulled her onto his lap, holding her tightly against him. "Sam can't know the truth, Taz." She looked up at him, her eyes huge with fear.

"We'll make sure he doesn't." Taz took her hand gently and looked at it. The sliver of glass was embedded in her hand. "Come on. We need to get that glass out."

Helping her up, he led her to the sink. As gently as he could, he tried to get the glass out but couldn't.

"Here, let me." She pulled her hand away. "I've got fingernails."

Her voice sounded so lost and sad, it drove him insane. She didn't deserve this, and neither did Sam. He watched as she pulled at the glass a few times before finally capturing it. Reaching over, he turned on the faucet as she stuck her hand underneath, washing out the wound. Blood and water mixed before disappearing down the drain.

"I'm going to kill him," he vowed, realizing he had spoken aloud.

Slowly, her head tilted up as she stared at him.

"Not if I get to him first," she also vowed, her hand still under the water. "But if for some reason I don't, and he gets me first, swear to me that you will not let him have Sam."

"That's not going to happ—"

"Swear it, Taz." She grabbed his arms with both hands and squeezed as if her life depended on his answer. The journal pinched his skin between them. "Swear it!"

"I swear." Taz pulled her to him, but in his mind, he

knew that would never come to pass. Nothing would happen to her; it was his own vow to himself. "Come on. Let's get you out of here."

Leda cupped her hands and rinsed her face, then washed her mouth out. Turning off the water, she glanced back up at him. "There's one more thing I need to do."

Before she could reach down around the glass to get her picture, he pulled her back and picked it up for her. "I've got it."

As they approached the door, she stopped. "Thank you," she whispered as she glanced up at him. "For being here for me."

Taz leaned down and kissed her gently. "I wouldn't be anywhere else."

~

Tears filled Leda's eyes, but she kept them from spilling over at his words. Instead, she took a deep breath for what she was about to do.

Walking out of the bathroom, she looked into the three serious faces who stared at her.

"Where's Malcolm?"

"I sent him outside to get himself under control." Garrett frowned as he searched her face. "You okay?"

She could lie and say yes, but they'd know it was a lie. "No, I'm not." She shook her head. "I know we need to get out of here, but there's something I need to do first."

"That's fine." Dell nodded, then pulled her in for a hug. "Whatever you need to do, we're here for you. They're already transporting some of your pack to Lee County."

"Thank you." She hugged him back, then was pulled into Garrett's arms, and Hunter's.

"I kinda liked you with short hair." Hunter grinned as he peered down at her after pulling away. "Not. Where in the hell did you get that godawful thing?"

Leda rolled her eyes, then reached in her back pocket where she'd stored the wig. "I need my wig." She frowned, looking around her.

"Believe me, you don't," Hunter teased, but when Leda looked a little panicked, he stopped her from searching herself. "Hey, I'll find it. Calm down."

"Okay." She nodded, knowing they didn't understand, but she needed that wig. Hunter stepped away. "Has the house been searched? The basement?"

"Everything's in place, now that you've gotten the closet cleared out." Dell frowned at her, letting her know he wasn't happy she'd gone alone upstairs before it was checked out.

With a nod, Leda took hold of Taz's hand and led them down the stairs until she stood in front of the basement door. Opening it, she stood for a second and took a deep breath as she headed down, but Taz stopped her and squeezed in front of her while Dell and Garrett followed from the rear.

They quietly trailed Taz until they reached a wall. Stepping around him, Leda stared at the shelves now full of her uncle's stuff. Putting her mother's journal safely in the waistband of her jeans, she swiped her uncle's belongings off the bottom shelf and onto the floor. She proceeded to do that until only the upper shelves remained. Satisfaction thrummed through her at destroying his things, making her feel more in control.

Stepping back, she grasped the small handle that had been discreetly placed at the bottom shelf and pulled it out. With a tug, she stepped back as the shelves, as one, rose toward the ceiling, the rest of her uncle's stuff falling to the floor as it rose higher. Once the shelf was fully opened, it revealed the paper-thin fake wall.

"I'll be damned," Garrett breathed behind her.

When she pushed and the door didn't give, a smile lit her face. Her uncle had no clue of its existence. She used her shoulder, but it only gave a little bit. Taz moved her aside and used both hands to push the door open. Leda reached in and flipped a switch as hundreds of little light bulbs lit the way deep into the tunnel.

"This is how we escaped," she said proudly. "My father worked on this himself for years because he didn't want anyone to know about it. It saved Sam and me that night. My mom shoved us in here, said her goodbyes and then lowered the shelves. I heard everything until I knew I had to run for Sam's sake."

"How far does it go?" Dell stepped in, having to duck, as did all the men.

"A mile, I think." Leda thought about how long it seemed that night as she carried Sam. "The lights were burnt out more than halfway through. We came out right at the other side of town where the creek runs."

As the men studied her father's work, she stepped out, looking around. Seeing large boxes, she walked that way and pulled one open. It was full of jewelry, all kinds of pieces. Going to the next box, she opened it and frowned. This one was filled with guns. Reaching down, she picked one up. It was unloaded.

Hearing the shelf being lowered, she looked that way. "No!"

Garrett stopped and glanced over his shoulder at her.

"I want the bastard to know my father and mother outsmarted him in the end." Once again, she looked into the tunnel, then returned her focus to the boxes. "Leave it, please."

The guys joined her without saying a word and started searching with her. "Looks like he's got a lot of stolen merchandise down here." Garrett frowned, then walked farther back on the other side of the cellar. "Same thing back here."

Knowing what she had to do, she gave the basement one last look before she headed toward the stairs. Climbing up, she waited for Taz to pass her, knowing the routine. It was fine. She wasn't in a great state of mind to protect herself.

She stepped into the kitchen, where her family had so many great moments, as well as a few heartaches, then turned away in distaste; it was filled with booze, overflowing ashtrays for the ones who bothered to use them, and dirty dishes piled in the sink.

Without a second thought, she headed toward the front door, down the porch steps and then turned to look at the house without concentrating on the bodies littering the ground. Her mind made up, she glanced around at everyone who remained staring at her. She saw Hunter holding her wig. When she held out her hand, he walked over and passed it to her. She took the picture of herself out of Taz's hand and tossed them both on the ground.

"Anyone have a match and some gasoline?" she said loudly as she stared at what used to be her home.

"Blaze!" Jared, who stood to her left, called out. She glanced his way. "We have something better than matches and gas."

Blaze moved to stand next to her. "You sure about this?"

Leda nodded, noticing Blaze looked toward Sloan, who gave him a nod, and then to Dell, who also gave his approval.

"Best step back a bit," he warned, and waited until Taz pulled her a safe distance away.

Leda watched as a ball of fire danced in Blaze's hand. She glanced up to his flaming eyes, knowing he was waiting for her. She nodded.

Blaze reared back his hand and threw the fireball toward the house, with many more following until it went up in flames. The whole group watched it burn.

"This the only one?" Blaze asked as he stepped back next to Leda.

As she watched the only home she had ever known burn, she glanced down at her picture and wig, then back up again. "Yeah, this is the only one."

Burning her home while leaving the rest intact would show her uncle that this was an attack against him and no one else. Even when this was over, she didn't think she could live in the house she had loved without the memories of what happened there. This whole town held good memories, but also nightmares that she didn't think any of them could overcome. As much as it hurt, she watched the only thing that had once belonged to her family burn. It was time to start with a clean slate, somewhere that didn't hold a nightmare around every corner.

Reaching over, she took Taz's hand, which wasn't far from hers, then turned her back, knowing this wasn't the end of her past. She'd just made sure of it.

"This is going to leave one hell of a message," the vamp called Sid said as they all strode away through the now empty shifter town.

"I'm counting on it," Leda whispered. She had been changed forever, and there was only one person to blame for that. Soon, they would come face-to-face, and she would be more than ready.

CHAPTER 16

$\mathcal{T}$he ride back to Lee County seemed to take forever. When Steve, with his minivan full of people, had dropped Taz off at his bike, there wasn't even a question that Leda was coming with him. Actually, he was really worried about her. It was as if she were on autopilot, only speaking when spoken to. She had sat on his lap to make room for someone else in the van, and he'd felt her body shivering.

He followed Steve until they passed the Lee County sign before turning off. Finding a secluded area, he slowed his bike to a stop.

"What are we doing?" Leda asked, her head still pressed against his back as she held onto him.

"I need to make sure you're okay," Taz answered honestly.

"I'm fine." Her response seemed automatic. Before he

could speak, Leda laughed. "But we both know that's a lie."

With an aching heart, Taz got off the bike before he helped her. Leda stretched and rubbed her legs before looking up at him.

"How about 'I'm fine, all things considered.'" Leda shrugged thoughtfully, as if trying her words out herself. "Yeah, that sounds better."

"If I could change any of this for you, I would." Taz picked a strand of her hair from the corner of her mouth and moved it behind her ear. "But that wouldn't solve the issue."

"No, it wouldn't." Leda sighed, then rubbed her eyes. "But at this point, I might just let you take care of it all, and I'll go hide in some dark hole until it's over."

He offered her a small smile. "That wouldn't be something you would do."

Shaking her head, Leda threw her head back. "Why wasn't he there, Taz?" As she stared at the sky, he knew she waited for his answer, but he didn't have one. "What if I made a huge mistake taking them from their homes? He's going to come for me. I made damn sure of that. I left Lee County alone because I didn't want to involve anyone. Now I've got innocent people involved." She shook her head, her voice catching. "I miss them, Taz. I miss them so much. My dad would have known what to do. Why did this happen? Did I make a mistake?"

She started to unravel before him, and hell, who could

blame her? He was still reeling at what he had learned and couldn't even imagine her feelings.

"Listen to me." Taz gently tugged her hair, bringing her face to meet his. "None of those people had to leave. They wanted to leave, and you gave them that freedom to choose. And I know you miss your parents, I understand, but you have people who care about you, who are beside you in this by their choice."

"Are you here by choice, Taz? Or is it some obligation you feel you have for me?" Leda whispered as her eyes searched his.

"Do you really have to ask me that question to know the truth?" Taz growled, pulling her into his arms. His hand gripped her jaw, bringing her mouth to his. The kiss was possessive but full of feelings that couldn't be denied. When their lips parted, Taz pulled away the barest of inches. "My life belongs to you. What you feel, I feel. What you experience, I experience. We are one, and I would lay my life down for you."

A tear slipped down her cheek as a soft smile curved her lips. "You love me?"

"Yes, I love you." Taz ran his thumb along the bottom of her lip. "More than you can ever imagine. From the first day I saw you, I knew you would be mine."

"I love you." Leda kissed him softly, then wrapped her arms around his neck, pulling him close. After a few minutes, she sighed. "Sorry about my little pity party."

Taz grinned against the top of her head. "If anyone deserves a pity party right now, it's you." He pulled back to look down at her. "But we need to go before they send out a search party. I just wanted to make sure you were okay and give you a minute before you see Sam."

"I can't wait to see him." Leda nodded with a large grin, but then it began to slip as memories clouded her eyes.

He could see Leda's excitement fade as thoughts entered her mind, which pissed him off. Her bastard of an uncle had ruined a family, and that was something he definitely wouldn't get away with, even if Taz had to hunt the motherfucker down himself.

"Hey, nothing has changed." He led her toward the bike, then leaned down and whispered against her ear, "He's still your brother. Nothing changes that, ever. I will protect him with my life, as I will you. You are a package deal that I will cherish."

Leda looked at him thoughtfully. "I never knew you were so sweet."

Neither did he, which surprised him, but when it came to her, he did things that were so out of his ordinary that nothing shocked him when it came to Leda and his feelings for her. "Just don't tell anyone, especially Steve."

The first chuckle he'd heard from her since they were reunited escaped her lips, and he would make damn sure he heard it more often. Just like he had before all of this happened.

Not even half an hour later, they pulled into Beattyville. There was a crowd waiting near Garrett's house. Taz pulled up and parked, but Leda's eyes were searching for Sam. Seeing him push his way through the crowd of people, she jumped off the bike, tripping and going down on her knees.

"Dammit, Leda." Taz helped her up just as Sam slammed into her, knocking her back down.

"Leda!" Sam cried, burying his head in her neck and nearly choking her to death. The sobs that shook his body tore her apart. Guilt rushed through her for leaving him.

"Hey now." Leda tried to pull him away so she could see him, but he held her even tighter, making it impossible. "I'm back, Sam. Come on now. Let me see you. I wasn't gone that long."

"Y-y-you were go-go-gone forever." Sam sniffed into her hair. "Pl-pl-ease."

"I won't." She squeezed him with her promise, knowing what he was saying despite not voicing his fears. "I'm sorry, Sam."

She glanced up to see her and Sam's pack moving toward her and her brother. With Taz's help, she stood, with Sam still wrapped around her. Soon everyone surrounded them, giving her and Sam hugs and thank-yous for her help. The responsibility she now had on her shoulders was so overwhelming it terrified her. These people had left their home—in hell, but still their homes —to follow her. Did she deserve such trust?

As soon as she thought she couldn't take it, she felt Taz at her back with his hand on her shoulder.

"Okay, everyone!" Dell walked through, taking control. "We are finding arrangements for all of you. Just be patient."

John Biel stepped forward. She remembered him well. He was a good friend of her father's, but somewhat older. "I'm good with a hammer," he said, his eyes leaving Leda and going straight to Dell. "I can build most anything I set my mind to. I'm not here for a hand-out. I thank you all for what you've done and would love to be a part of an honest pack." Lots of murmurs of agreement sprang up from the group of her old pack. "We are loyal and have already had a discussion of what we can offer."

Leda smiled as she looked around at all the hopeful, yet ravaged and tired faces.

"We want our pack to grow and flourish," Dell replied, glancing at Garrett, who nodded. "And we don't turn down loyalty and hard work, that's for sure."

John beamed with pride and gratitude, as did the others of her pack. Proud, she offered John a big smile. They were good people who deserved so much more than what her uncle had offered them.

John then turned to Leda.

"Thank you for what you did for us today." John glanced at Sam, then back to her. "We didn't know what happened to you. I'm so sorry for your loss. Your father was the best alpha any pack could ever have, and your mother was a real sweet lady."

Feeling her throat tighten at his words and the agreements coming from those behind him, she swallowed hard. "Thank you," she managed to say and knew if she said any more, she would be blubbering all over the place.

"Hey, everyone," Janna called out. "I know you all are hungry. We have a lot of food ready at the coffee shop."

A few stayed behind to thank Leda personally, but soon the crowd faded away toward the coffee shop. Finally, Sam loosened his grip and wiggled to get down, then looked way up at Taz.

"I knew y-you'd sa-sa-save her." Sam grabbed Taz around the legs, giving them a big hug. Then he stepped back, gazing at Taz with a look of hero worship.

Her heart melted as Taz knelt in front of Sam and put his hand on his shoulder. "I will always save Leda when she needs saving." Taz gave him a nod, and Sam gave him a nod back. "Now go get yourself something to eat so you can get big and strong, because I might need your help."

Sam gave him a high five, then took off running. He stopped and turned to look at Leda. "Don't leave." He didn't stutter.

"I won't." She crossed her heart. "I promise."

She slowly stood as her breathing came in rapid spurts. "He can't find him, Taz," she whispered, but Dell and Garrett were close enough to hear her words.

"He won't," Taz said, his voice hard and sure.

"Nothing will happen to Sam, Leda." Garrett finally

took her into his arms, giving her a hug. "Nothing will happen to you either. You're protected here."

Leda nodded, not feeling so sure. She knew these men could protect her and Sam, but she also knew her uncle better than they did.

Her eyes found Jamie. She stood with Devon, who carried a huge plate of food. Jamie waved her over as Malcolm came walking toward them slowly.

"Jamie wants you," he said, his eyes not meeting hers. "And we both know how Jamie gets when she doesn't get what she wants."

A smile broke over Leda's face. "Believe me, I remember well." She glanced at Taz, who was glaring at Malcolm before he looked down at her.

"Go ahead. I'll be over in a second."

She started to pass Malcolm but stopped, then gave him a hug. "I know you were doing what you thought best for your sister. I forgive you."

Malcolm looked at her in surprise but remained silent.

"I've always looked at you like my big brother, and that hasn't changed, nor will it." She wanted to make it damn clear that she had no feelings other than that toward him. "And if you ever think to turn on me again, know that these three men behind me will kill you, plus a few more who aren't present at the moment. This is my family now, and it can be yours if you get your shit straight."

"Thank you." Malcolm cleared his throat, then went to hug her, but he stopped when Taz growled.

"Don't even think about it," Taz warned without taking a step, but everyone knew he was ready to pounce. "She may have forgiven you, but I haven't."

CHAPTER 17

*T*az glared at Malcolm long enough to make the man uncomfortable. He then watched Leda go sit with Jamie, noticing she bypassed the food. That was something he would take care of as soon as he got some answers to questions that had been bothering him. And he wanted the answers without Leda being there. Right or wrong, he would let her know in his own time if he felt she needed to.

"When is this bastard supposed to be back, and where has he been?" Taz's voice drew the interest of Dell and Garrett. Most of the Warriors were still there and had walked toward them. Hunter and Marcus also arrived.

"He doesn't always say where he's going, but at the earliest, tomorrow." Malcolm looked him straight in the eyes as he answered, but that meant nothing to Taz. He'd had people lie to his face many times.

"Is he searching for Leda?" Taz continued.

"He's always looking for Leda." Again, no hesitation in his answer.

"Why the bounty only on Leda and not Sam?" Garrett took a turn at Malcolm.

Steve and Adam walked over, both with big plates of food, Steve glancing at Taz. "Garrett and Dell filled Sloan in on the situation and then told us." He frowned at Malcolm.

"And don't pull the age card." Sloan also appeared. "Because we all know in our world that's bullshit."

"Leda is the one who's a threat to Allen, or should I say whoever she mates with." Malcolm focused on Taz. "Sam is not the threat, because he's not Jason Kingsman's son, and it can be proven."

"How?" Dell asked, doubt evident in his voice.

"The journal," Taz said as his eyes once again found Leda, seeing it sticking out of her waistband.

"The journal." Malcolm nodded. "Allen tore that place apart looking for that damn journal but never found it. I always knew where it was. Right under his nose."

"How did he even know there was a journal?" Sloan asked as everyone else listened closely.

Malcolm also looked toward Leda with a sad smile. "Leda's mother taunted him at the very end of her life." Malcolm got a faraway look in his eyes, and Taz wondered if the man had lost a little bit of his mind somewhere. "She told him about the journal and that one day what he had done would come back to haunt him. He had us all looking for the damn thing, but I knew exactly where it was because my mother told me. It's been untouched since the day Jewel hid it, taped to her dresser mirror.

"Where is it now?" That came from Katrina, who stood with Blaze's arm wrapped around her.

"Leda has it." Taz nodded her way.

"Where it belongs," Katrina added before kissing Blaze on the cheek and walking toward Leda and Jamie.

Devon jogged over just as Katrina left. "Hey, Jamie is asking if anyone saw that guy Minor." Devon glanced around.

"I searched but didn't see him among the others." Malcolm frowned.

"He the one who came out on the porch first?" Blaze asked, his arms crossed over his chest. When Malcolm nodded, Blaze shook his head. "I don't remember seeing him after everything went down."

"If he got away, I can guarantee you Allen knows what went down." Malcolm looked around at all of them. "And it won't be long before he responds."

Unsurprised, Taz had figured it wouldn't be long anyway since Leda had pretty much left her calling card. He hadn't liked what she'd done, only because it put a bigger target on her; then again, she did have a fifty-thousand-dollar bounty on her head. Jesus, just the thought had him sweating. It was a lot of money.

"Did he just keep the bounty among his men?" Taz asked, hoping the answer was yes.

"Yeah, because he could control it," Malcolm replied, then nodded toward where Sam was, who'd just run past. "He didn't want a chance of Sam getting hurt and knew they were together. He could order his men what to do, but anyone not loyal to him wouldn't care if a little kid got killed in the process of a big payday."

"So no one in the pack knows about Sam?" Taz continued to question, not caring how long it took.

"No," Malcolm replied, then frowned. "In his own strange way, I think he wanted to have a father/son relationship with him. Then again, I don't really know. Allen had no clue that I knew as much as I did. I pledged my loyalty to him only because of the promise I made to my mom. I never thought one of his bastards would take my sister and make her his whore."

Devon sneered as he glanced at Malcolm. "Watch how you talk about Jamie."

"Don't tell me how to talk about my sister. Who the fuck are you, anyway?" Malcolm growled, taking a step toward Devon. "I'm not calling her a whore, asshole. I'm stating facts. He made my sister his fucking whore."

"Okay, guys!" Dell stepped between them. "We can't afford to fight with each other."

"I have no loyalty to that bastard." Malcolm glanced at Dell, then stared at Taz. "I will make up for my moment of weakness where my sister was concerned. It won't happen again."

Taz's eyes traveled to Adam, who gave him a nod. "Truth."

John Biel and a few other men walked up. "Excuse me," he said, looking a little uncomfortable. "We just wanted to let you know that we're more than willing to stand with you when the time comes. We should have done that tonight, but it's been a while since we had anyone on our side."

Taz really felt for the man and was damn proud to be part of the Lee County wolves when Dell slapped the man on the back. "We all need help sometimes." Dell glanced at the other men with respect. "We start training first thing tomorrow, and I expect every man who is able-bodied to be there, as well as any women."

Reaching out his hand, John shook Dell's. "You can count on us." The rest of the men shook Dell's hand as well. Before John walked off, he stopped. "Did she really burn down the main house?"

"She did," Taz answered, wondering how this was going to be taken by the other pack members.

John cleared his throat. "Good." His voice was full of emotion. "That house belonged to our true alpha. I hate that she had to do it, since she grew up in that house, but it needed to be done. Except...." Fear clouded the man's eyes.

"Except?" Dell frowned.

"Allen will never let that rest." He glanced at Taz, then away quickly. "He'll be out for blood. Her blood."

The men watched John walk away, no one saying a word

until Sloan broke the silence. "I can keep a few of my Warriors here," he offered Dell. "They can help you train some of the new men but also be here when shit hits, and from the sounds of it, you don't have long before that happens."

"I'd appreciate that." Dell wasn't a stupid man, and Garrett was nodding his approval as well. Even though Dell had taken over as alpha, Garrett was still there giving counsel, ensuring there was strength and support given. It helped make their pack strong. "Unfortunately, we have no idea how many he's going to come at us with."

"He'll come with as many as he can round up," Malcolm added, shifting nervously. "This is going to send him over the edge."

"Good," Taz sneered. "I hope he hurries the fuck up."

"I like him," he heard Sid say as he walked away toward Leda.

It was time she ate something.

Leda sat with Jamie, her mind going a mile a minute. She truly couldn't believe that she was sitting across from one of her best friends, and her old pack was actually here in Beattyville. Excitement, fear, and anxiety swarmed her senses, making her fidgety.

"It's going to be okay." Jamie was watching her closely. "I know what you're thinking."

"Oh, you do?" Leda gave her a lopsided grin. "Oh, amazing Jamie, what am I thinking?"

"That you made a mistake. You shouldn't have upset what we had." Jamie snorted as Leda's grin faded. "Told ya. I can still read you. Time hasn't changed that."

"I wanted to take care of this without involving anyone," Leda replied, then waved as Sam ran by with Pepper nipping at his butt.

"God, he's so damn cute." Jamie laughed, then turned serious as she looked around them. "It's been a long time since I saw Mrs. Watkins laugh and look healthy. Will you look at Mr. Watkins staring at his wife like a horny teenager? And Mason Jenson is walking a little taller with pride, not with slumped shoulders and fear. Then there's John Biel, who couldn't look anyone in the eye before, yet he walked straight toward vampire warriors and one of the baddest packs around to talk to them."

Leda's eyes followed Jamie's words as she observed what her friend spoke of.

"You did this, Leda." Jamie reached over and grabbed her arm, giving it a squeeze. "You. Did. This."

"But what if—" Leda started, but Jamie wouldn't let her finish.

"What if you never showed up? Hmm?" Jamie let go of her arm. "Let's talk about that, shall we, and take that bastard Allen—no, I will not call him my alpha because I never did—out of the equation. We would all be hiding in

148

our homes with our lights out, praying no one knocked on our door. Going about our day-to-day business, afraid to make the wrong move and be reported to him by one of his assholes. We lived in fear every minute of every day since your father was murdered, until today."

"Why didn't you run?" Leda turned back toward Jamie. "Others did, but you and Malcolm stayed."

"We couldn't leave our mom." Jamie smiled sadly. "The night everything happened, many of the younger ones scattered, never to be seen again, some even leaving their families with their blessing. Some stayed for different reasons, but every single one of them, both here and gone, mourned losing not only your mother and father but you and Sam."

"I just don't understand any of this, why it happened." Leda sighed, so tired her body and brain hurt.

"None of us understand, but it did happen, and I'm pregnant by a bastard I hope is dead." Jamie rubbed her bulging stomach. "None of that matters at the moment because we're free. You did the right thing, Leda, and I, for one, thank you for giving me and this little person a fighting chance."

"Oh, that reminds me!" Leda stood and started searching the crowd. She turned to take off but ran into something very hard. "Ouch."

"Whoa." Taz steadied her with one hand while his other held a plate of food. "Where you going? I got you a plate."

"I have to find Slade." She wrinkled her nose at the food. "And I'm not hungry."

"Are you hurt?" He frowned at her mention of needing Slade. "And you need to eat something."

"No, I'm not hurt, but I want him to see Jamie. She hasn't seen a doctor yet." Leda saw Jill and yelled out. "Hey, Jill."

"Oh, is the doctor that good-looking son of a gun." Jamie wiggled her eyebrows.

Jill came up just in time to hear Jamie. "Yes, ma'am." Jill grinned, then leaned down, whispering but loud enough that Taz and Leda could hear her. "He is yummy but can be a real grouch if you're his mate, which I am. Though he treats his patients like kings and queens."

Jamie laughed. "I'm Jamie." She shook Jill's hand. "And sorry. I swear I wasn't trying to pick up your man."

"Honey, all the women do." Jill winked at her. "But I'm a confident woman who will kick his ass if he even looks twice at a female."

"I like you." Jamie chuckled with a large grin.

"She hasn't seen a doctor yet," Leda explained as she sat back down. "Do you think Slade could help out?"

"How far along are you?" Jill frowned, glancing at her large stomach.

"Seven months, or at least close to that." Jamie sighed. "But the way I feel it seems about twelve months or longer."

"I'll go get him." Jill turned serious as she patted Jamie on the shoulder. "We'll get you and that little one taken care of."

Taz set the plate in front of Leda. "Eat." He sat next to her. "Or I'm telling Slade when he comes over here."

"I don't care." She shrugged, poking at the food with her fork. "Tell him."

Taz frowned, and then a large grin spread across his face. "Okay, I'll tell Steve."

"Ugh." Leda stabbed a piece of macaroni and put it in her mouth. Steve would drive her nuts until she ate. "That was a low blow, Taz."

"I know." He chuckled, putting his arm around her. "At least I found some use for the dumbass."

"Be nice." Leda kissed his cheek, then caught Jamie grinning at them.

"You guys are too cute." Jamie sighed, batting her eyelashes.

"Shut up." Leda tossed macaroni at her, but couldn't stop smiling while Taz pulled her close to him. Maybe, just maybe, things were going to be okay.

But deep inside she knew better.

CHAPTER 18

*L*eda lay in bed thinking of the past few hours. After Slade took Jamie up to Garrett's with Jill, Leda helped Ross and Janna clean up. More women jumped in to help, so it took them no time. Darla McClain was there, giving her dirty looks, but Leda was so over the high school drama. She wasn't in high school, and in the last twenty-four hours, she had grown way past Darla's maturity level, which made ignoring her so much easier.

She tossed and turned, her mind unable to settle. Every time she closed her eyes, she saw her house burning. She attempted to read her mother's journal but quickly put it aside, not ready yet. Everything was still too fresh, especially her worry for Sam that had tripled after seeing him. It was all too much.

Aggravated, she whipped the covers off and got out of bed, her mind going to Taz. She wanted to see him. Not knowing where he was, she quietly slipped out of her room and down the hall, only to have Garrett open their bedroom door.

"You okay?" he whispered, his eyes assessing her as a father would.

"Fine," she whispered over her shoulder. "Can't sleep."

Garrett nodded his understanding, then closed the door, allowing her to continue. After walking into the kitchen, she grabbed a glass of water.

"You okay?" Hunter's voice asked from behind her, making her choke on her water.

"You scared the crap out of me." She glanced in the living room to see Emily snuggled on the couch. "Go home and get some rest. She looks so uncomfortable."

"Let me worry about my woman, woman." Hunter smirked, leaning against the doorframe. "I'm damn proud of you, Leda."

"For what?" She wrinkled her nose. "Possibly bringing a madman onto your land set on revenge?"

He shrugged. "I'm always up for a fight." He straightened as his face turned serious. "Don't sell yourself short, kid. You were kickass today and gained the respect of many people. That's exactly what the daughter of a well-respected alpha would do."

Hunter disappeared back into the living room, allowing Leda to consider his words, the asshole. A smile played at the corner of her mouth as she shook her head.

She walked out the back door since she couldn't go out

the front with Emily sleeping in the living room. Once outside, she sat on the steps and looked toward the woods. She loved this time of night. It was so quiet, and her keen hearing could pick up all the nocturnal animals out and about, carrying on with their business.

A noise behind her sent her head snapping that way. Taz in his wolf form stood staring at her. He was beautiful and huge.

With a smile, she welcomed him with her arm outstretched. She had seen him in wolf form many times, and every time, he took her breath away. He stalked toward her as if she was prey, his eyes piercing into hers, asking her an unspoken question.

"I'm fine," she whispered as he stood towering over her. She leaned her head into his fur as her hand buried itself into the softness. "Can't sleep."

"You need your rest." His voice echoed in her mind.

Glancing back toward the woods, her wolf grew restless. "No, what I need to do is run." She stood, jumping off the back porch. She looked back over her shoulder with a smile at Taz.

"Leda!" The warning in his voice didn't faze her.

She hadn't shifted since before she'd left, and even though that was only a few weeks ago, it felt like a lifetime for her. She needed this. With a chuckle, she took off, shifting in midrun. Taz was much faster than her and was beside her within seconds. He nipped at her flank as he passed. She urged herself faster, doing the same to him.

Leda let him take the lead. She didn't care where they went, as long as it was in the woods. In all honesty, in her heart, she knew she would follow this man anywhere. As they leaped over fallen trees, the mud kicking up from their paws, their breath fogged the air as they ran. She loved this, loved her life, and decided right then and there that she was going to live it to the fullest. No matter what came her way, she had a support system that was unshakable.

Losing track of time when in her wolf form was easy for her to do. Actually, it had gotten her in a little bit of trouble in the past. After what seemed like hours, Taz stopped on a cliff overlooking the gorge. Leda stood next to him, both of them shaking out their fur after their run. Giving him a sideways look, she was in awe at the masculinity as he stared out over the land. She felt safe, but more importantly, she felt loved.

Pulling her eyes away from him, she glanced toward the sky. The stars were so close it felt like she could actually reach out and grab one.

Feeling his eyes on her, Leda dropped her head, looking at him in a submissive stance. Slowly, she moved her head, rubbing it along his. Desire shot through her, and she trembled as a low whine escaped her. She wanted him. With no doubts whatsoever in her mind, she wanted him, all of him.

Without hesitation, she shifted and stood before his wolf fully naked. They had seen each other as such many times, as it was their way. But now she didn't try to hide anything from him. She stood bare for his eyes only. His wolf gaze roamed her body as a low growl rumbled in his chest. The wolf took a step toward her but stopped. Their eyes locked as Taz shifted into human form. Just as his wolf had towered over her, so did the man. He was so close she could feel his heat, and it immediately set her soul on fire.

"Beautiful." His voice was a rough whisper, caressing her skin. Heat unfurled inside her, and she'd never felt more beautiful than that moment under his gaze.

Her eyes roamed over him as she stood before him. When her needy gaze stopped on his cock, her breath caught. He was hard and ready for her. She wanted to learn every single thing about this man who held her heart.

"You know everything there is to know about me." Her eyes rose to his. "And I have only recently learned your last name."

"There isn't much to know," Taz responded, his body still as stone. She wondered if he was having a hard time reining himself in like she was. She wanted nothing more than to pounce and to make him hers. But she held strong.

"I don't believe that." Leda shook her head with a smile. "I think there's a lot to learn about the man you are, and I want to know it all. The good, the bad, the women…," she teased, earning a frown from him.

"There are no women." His eyes narrowed. "Only you."

She gave him a "yeah right" look, but let it go. Tilting her head, she stared up at him. "I want to know the man

I'm giving myself to." She reached out, placing her hand over his heart. His skin was warm to the touch; his heart beating against her hand made her feel more alive. "I think that's only fair."

"My mother was a beautiful Irish woman who had a pure soul incomparable to anyone I have ever met." Taz's gaze never left hers.

"What was her name?"

"Aileen," he responded with a softness she had never heard in his voice before. "I miss her to this day."

"I'm sorry." Her hand moved from his chest, up his neck, cupping his jaw.

"My father was a full-blood Cherokee who liked his booze more than his family. Cusa Azure was a bastard when on the booze and tolerable when he wasn't." His eyes became clouded with memories. "But my mother loved him, and in his own messed-up way, he loved her."

"Wait a minute." Leda frowned. "Your last name is Whelan. But your father's name is Azure."

"Not many know my last name." Taz eyed her with a cocked eyebrow. "How did you know it?"

"Oh, I have my ways," Leda teased as she took a step closer. "Is he still alive?"

"Don't know," Taz replied, with absolutely no emotion in his voice. "After my mom died, my sister, Dawn, and I left while he was passed out in his chair. We finally found a pack to take us in. The alpha fell in love with my sister, and then…." He leaned down as he clasped her hand on his jaw in his.

"Then what?" she whispered, her eyes going to his lips, then back to his eyes.

"I came looking for you," he answered against her lips.

His words melted her, completely made her weak to the point that her knees buckled. His strong arm wrapped around her waist, pulling her against him as his mouth ravaged her. Leda was hyperaware of their naked bodies pressed together, and it felt so right. Her skin was sensitive, sending the most amazing sensation through her body. Her arms wrapped tightly around him as if she couldn't get enough, and she couldn't.

"We need to stop." Taz pulled his mouth from hers, but after he spoke the words, he kissed her again.

"No, we don't," she breathed against his lips as her hands began to roam his body. He started doing the same until he groaned and pushed her away from him.

"Leda" was all he said, his breathing deep and rapid.

"What?" She frowned, then tried to grab onto him again, but he kept her at arm's length.

"We really need to stop." His eyes defied his words as they once again roamed her body. As if realizing what he was doing, he shook his head. "Dammit, Leda. You're not ready for this."

That was like a cold slap to the face. Her head even snapped back at his words. "Says who? You?" She frowned, taking a step back. "You know, I'm getting really sick and tired of people telling me what to do and what they think I'm ready for. It was one of the reasons I went out on my own."

"Listen, I didn't mean it the way it sounded." Taz went to reach for her, but she moved out of the way. "But are you really ready for this? I know you've never... you know."

"Had sex? Made love?" Leda snorted with a roll of her eyes. "You can't even say the words. You sure you're ready?"

Taz growled at her, his eyes narrowing. "Oh, I'm ready."

"Then do something about it." Leda spread her arms wide. "Or do I have too much baggage for you? Is that what this is about?"

That time when Taz reached out to grab her, she wasn't fast enough to move out of the way. She found herself once again plastered against his body, exactly where she wanted to be. He cupped her jaw, forcing her gaze to his.

"Any baggage you have, I will carry on my shoulders." His mouth came down hard on hers. His hands were everywhere, and she couldn't get enough. "Are you sure, Leda?" he asked between kissing down her neck, across her collarbone, but before he went lower, he gazed up at her.

"I've never been surer of anything in my life," she whispered, then guided his head to her breast that waited bare for his touch. "I love you, Taz. I trust you."

She moaned as Taz took control. Her head fell back as

she welcomed the intense feelings this man evoked in her body. She gave herself to him freely, without any doubts or hesitation. It was the perfect time and perfect place with the perfect man. What more could she ever ask for?

CHAPTER 19

*T*az felt like a kid having his first time with a female. He started out a fumbling mass of nerves, but after a mental talk down, he swore to himself that this woman in his arms would know exactly who she belonged to. She deserved the best from him, especially for her first time, and he would not let her down. Never would he let her down.

Her skin tasted sweet and salty, her scent of desire nothing like he had ever experienced in his life. Taz had wanted nothing in his life more than her, and to think she was giving herself to him freely had him soaring with a need that scared him.

She touched him like an experienced lover, but he knew different. She was not experienced, and that made her touch that much sweeter. Leda wanted him without reservation or fear. A little timid at first, but the more he tuned her body with his touch, she became bolder, and he liked it. Liked it a lot.

"Taz," she moaned, her lower body pushing toward him, searching for something she didn't understand yet, but what he knew so well.

Running his hand down her stomach, over her hip to her ass, then back to the sweet spot, he touched her gently with one finger, letting her get used to the feel of him in her most private area. He was determined to make this special for her, and by damn, he wouldn't fail.

At least that was his thought until she unexpectedly ran her hand along his painfully hard cock. Clenching his teeth, he allowed her to explore his body, as he did the same.

"You feel so good," she whispered, kissing his chest. He groaned as she looked down, watching her own hand gripping him.

Talking himself down, again, he braced himself and let her have a moment of freedom. He tried to take that time to scan their surroundings since they were out in the open. If he wasn't careful, he could easily leave them defenseless just from being so distracted by her touch. Plus separating himself from what her small hand was doing to him gave him a chance to control not only the man but his wolf, who was excitedly restless.

Feeling her lips close to his navel, he glanced down as she sank to her knees.

"Can I taste it?"

"Fuck!" he growled, grasping her shoulders before she

could do just that. If her lips went anywhere near his cock, he knew he would lose control and explode. "Let's save that for next time." Even the thought of her taking him in her mouth had his dick throbbing painfully.

She gave him a pout but took his hand as she stood, placing his calloused palm on her breast. "I like when you touch me."

He pinched her puckered nipple between his fingers. His heart pounded as hard as his cock. To find his mate was one thing, but to find a mate who was sexual without experience was a score not many found. Even though their kind were sexual by nature, sometimes between two people, it just wasn't there. Oh, they would fuck to appease their appetite, and he'd done that plenty, but to totally enjoy each other in so many different ways was something he'd always wanted. With Leda, he'd found that, but today, her first time, he would take it slowly. Even if it fucking killed him.

"Why do you get to taste me but I don't get to taste you?" She touched her other breast, offering it to him. "Doesn't seem quite fair."

He knew she was ready for him. He could smell her. The way her body moved and wiggled told him her pussy was throbbing. Taz's jaw ticked as he ground his teeth together, trying to keep control. "Soon you can do what-ever you want to me and my body," he said through clenched teeth. Taking her down to the ground, he posi-tioned her on her hands and knees. "But first, before I lose all control, I'm going to make you mine in all ways a man claims his woman."

Taz ran his hands up and down her back, past her nice firm ass, and then slid his finger inside her slowly. Oh yeah, she was definitely ready for him, slick and wet. He slipped a second finger inside, using his body to keep her still—his chest against her back with enough pressure to keep her locked in position.

"I can't see you." Leda tried to look at him over her shoulder. "I want to see you, touch you." Her voice came out in gasps of pleasure as he continued to use his hand, getting her ready for him.

"Soon, but this way you will feel less pain for your first time," Taz whispered against her ear. "Trust me."

"I do," she whispered with emotion. "More than anyone, I trust you, Taz."

Knowing he couldn't take much more before he lost all control, he asked her one more time. "Are you sure, *uwoduhi*?"

"I love you," she responded, her gaze meeting his over his shoulder. "I've been ready for a long time."

"As have I." Taz positioned himself at her opening as he straightened so both hands were free. Grasping her hips, he paused for only a second, hating the pain she was about to feel, but soon it would just be a distant memory. To know he was the first made him want to scream to the sky, but he refrained. His wolf was doing enough howling in his head that he felt somewhat restrained as a man.

With one solid thrust, he was buried inside her. When he felt the resistance of her virginity and then broke through, he growled with pure male satisfaction. Remaining still inside her was the hardest thing he had ever done in his life, but he was giving her body time to adjust.

She moaned, and he couldn't tell if it was from pleasure or pain.

"Are you okay?"

"Is that it?" Her voice sounded disappointed, and he cursed but grinned at her question.

"No, not at all." He reached around, plucking at her hardened nipple before cupping her full breast with a squeeze.

"Thank God," she hissed, that time he could tell in pleasure. "Then yeah, I'm good."

Shocked that he could love this woman any more than he already did, he moved inside her, only small amounts at a time. Her head hung low as she grew accustomed to the movement inside her. Soon her body became curious, as did the woman, and she rocked with him.

Watching himself slide in and out of her was more than he could stand, so he looked away. "Damn," he hissed as she slammed back against him. "Careful, don't hurt yourself."

"I need more, Taz." She cried out when he stopped and pulled out of her. "No!"

He flipped her over and she spread her legs, silently begging him to slide back inside her. He did so immediately and pumped harder and faster. Her full breasts bounced with each thrust and he couldn't look away, mesmerized. Taz's cock swelled inside her even more. Putting his hand flat on her stomach above her pussy, he found the sweet nub with his thumb just begging to be touched. He needed to move her along; he only had so much control. He had dreamed of this moment, pleasured himself many times thinking of being wrapped in her wet heat, but now that it was a reality, he was about to lose all control. And no man worth a woman like Leda would come before her.

When she looked up, their eyes met, and hers begged for something she didn't understand, at least not yet. He would teach her things about her body and very soon, and without a doubt, he knew she would be a damn enthusiastic student.

"Come on, Leda." His whisper was hissed. "Let go. Give me everything you have."

She met him thrust for thrust. Her mouth opened, but nothing came out. She was on edge.

He flicked her nub hard and fast, enough to cause pleasure with a tiny bit of pain. She grabbed her own breast, trying to find release, and he loved every single fucking minute of it. Watching her play with her own tits was almost too much for him to take. Grabbing her hands, he clasped them together with his larger one and trapped them over her head as he pounded into her. Her legs wrapped around his waist, his free hand going underneath her ass. His legs took the weight and balance as he fucked her hard. He had lost it. This girl who freely gave herself to him as her first had caused him to lose all control.

"Jesus!" he growled as his body pumped into hers and she finally broke over the edge. Her scream of pleasure echoed around him as he shot his cum into her over and over again until they were both spent.

They lay together, neither saying a word as they tried to regain themselves. He was still inside her, semihard, and felt her pussy spasm around him. He moved slightly, causing her to moan with pleasure.

"Can we do it again?" she begged, greedily angling her hips.

He raised his body off her and moved inside her, shocked when his cock began to harden. That time, he took her slowly, kissing her until she spasmed again and his cock emptied inside her for the second time in less than five minutes.

"Wow," she whispered, looking at him in awe. "I didn't think guys could do it again so quickly."

Her words penetrated his sex-crazed mind, making him frown. "And how the hell would you know something like that?"

She gave him a flirty smile. "Girls talk about sex, you know."

He chuckled, pulled out of her slowly and moved partially off her so he could stare down at her. "It's usually different with men, but you have a way of bringing the best out of me."

Leda laughed, then kissed his chin. "That was... amazing."

"It was," he agreed, moving a strand of hair from her eye. "You're going to be sore. I should have been gentler."

"Ah, no you shouldn't have." Leda sat up, glaring down at him. "What just happened was perfect, so don't ruin it."

With his heart speeding up at the gorgeous, fiery woman before him, he grabbed her and kissed her hard. "You are mine."

"And you are mine," she countered with a sigh.

"I am yours." He gave her a nod and pulled her into his lap as they waited to watch the sunrise before it was time to face reality, as well as four men who looked upon Leda as a father and brothers. He just may get his ass kicked today.

Taz held her tightly against him. It would be totally worth it—*she* was totally worth it. Nothing and no one would keep them apart now.

"I love you." At her whispered words, his heart soared.

"I love and cherish you," he whispered back, feeling content with his woman wrapped in his arms.

CHAPTER 20

*L*eda couldn't wipe the smile off her face. They had stopped at one of the shelters where clothes had been stashed before heading back home.

When Garrett's house came into view, Taz asked, "You nervous?" as he helped her over the wooden fence.

"Nope." She grinned as they walked around the small pond. "You?"

"Depends." Taz raised her hand, placing a kiss on her knuckles. "Whether they come at me one at a time or all at once."

Just as they rounded the side of the house, the back door slammed open and out walked Garrett, followed by Hunter, Marcus, Dell, Steve, Jared, Slade, Blaze, and Sid. All of them had different expressions on their face.

"Go in the house," Taz whispered out of the corner of his mouth.

"No, I'm standing beside you," Leda argued, noticing only the wolves looked pissed. The rest were grinning like idiots. Steve wore the biggest cheesy grin of them all as he leaned against the porch rail. He held up his hand, giving them the naughty finger shake. Leda was about to give him a finger of her own until Garrett's bellow stopped her.

"Where in the hell have you been?"

"Garrett," Janna's voice warned from inside the house.

"She's been with me," Taz answered, not offering anything more.

"That's all you got?" Hunter growled, his eyes narrowed. "She's been with you?"

"That's all you're going to get," Taz replied, and Leda actually flinched.

"Taz, maybe we should, erm—"

Hunter started down the steps, but Marcus stopped him. "Cool down, brother."

"Leda, get in the house." When Leda remained next to Taz's side, staring and defying Garrett, he reared his head back. "Now!"

She jumped but stood her ground. "No." Her voice shook a little, so she cleared it. "No!" she said louder, with more authority.

Janna walked outside, pushing the men out of the way.

"Leda, come inside and let the boys talk." She held out her hand, waving her on. "Come on."

Leda glared at Garrett before turning. She tiptoed up, kissing Taz on the mouth. Taz kissed her back, even going as far as wrapping his arm around her waist, pulling her to him. She fell into the kiss, wishing she didn't have an audience and that they were back on the clifftop.

After reluctantly pulling away, she stomped toward the porch, stopping in front of Garrett, Hunter, and Marcus. "Hurt him and I will never talk to you again," she warned, then pushed past them, going into the house. She grinned when she heard Janna's warning.

"Play nice or don't come back inside," Janna hissed, following behind Leda.

Leda peered around at Ross, Emily, Katrina, Jill, and Jamie, who were all grinning at her. "You mated!" Jamie squealed excitedly as she ran up and hugged her.

"Oh damn." Emily grinned as she also hugged her. "Congrats. I just hope Taz is getting the same reception out there."

Raised voices clearly indicated that was not the case. All the women looked at each other, then rushed toward the windows to watch.

"I have to go out there." Leda started for the door, but Janna stepped in her way, shaking her head.

"Let your man be the man and answer up." Jill gave her a knowing wink. "He can take care of himself."

"Ah, he's a little outnumbered." Leda frowned, not feeling right letting Taz take all the heat. She had a say in what happened between them.

"For now he is," Ross said as she looked over Jamie's head, giving her a knowing grin. "If he needs saving, we'll have his back."

Janna gave her a tight hug. "He's a lucky guy."

"I'm the lucky one." Leda hugged her back, then looked out the window. Her eyes found Taz, and he didn't look happy.

~

Taz stood his ground, knowing this confrontation was going to happen. He didn't expect it this soon, but then again, that was his misjudgment. He would stand up to a thousand men for Leda without a second thought. Because of his respect for the men now glaring at him, he wished it would have happened differently, but it hadn't. He hadn't planned on mating with Leda that night, but he had, and he wouldn't change it if his life depended on it.

"What do you have to say for yourself?" Hunter started on him as soon as the door closed behind the women. He came off the porch to stand almost directly in front of him. "She has a madman after her, a huge fucking bounty on her head, and all you can think of is getting in—"

"Don't say it." Taz's eyes narrowed in warning; his words came out in a growl.

"Oh shit," Steve said, but Taz ignored him.

"—her pants." Hunter finished, as if daring Taz to do anything about it.

Taz did instantly. He punched out, hitting Hunter square in the mouth. "Don't ever talk about her like that." Taz was too busy running his mouth to see the counter-punch coming his way. It hit him like a brick, sending him stumbling backward. He shook his head, then wiped the blood from his mouth with a smile. "That all you got?"

Curses from the porch surrounded Taz and Hunter as they went for each other. Taz heard Leda screaming, but was too busy dodging blows and getting hit. They ended up in the water.

"Stop them!" Leda screamed, with Janna doing the same thing.

"Let them get it out of their systems." Garrett's voice carried to Taz.

"Leda, get back inside," Taz ordered between punches. One hit him in the jaw, and he heard a tooth crack. "Fuck!"

"Stop." Leda trudged through the water trying to get to them. Taz leaned back and kicked Hunter in the stomach, sending him flying back and under the water. He grabbed Leda, picked her up and sent her out of the water to safety before Hunter was grabbing him and dragging him backward. "No!"

"Oh, for shit's sake." Jill stomped down to the water's edge.

"Jill!" Slade warned. "Stay out of it."

She snorted. "Yeah, when have I ever stayed out of anything?"

"Never!" Steve answered.

"Shut it, Steve," Jill hissed.

Taz was trying to keep an eye on Leda while he was fighting for his life. He heard and saw everything. "Steve, get her out of here."

"Dude, I've wanted to see you get your ass kicked for a long damn time." Steve grinned, making Taz growl. "I ain't missing this for nothing."

Before Jill could do her thing and separate them, Hunter yelled, "Shit, is that a snake?"

"Why yes, yes it is." Katrina grinned, then winked at both Hunter and Taz, who looked her way. "I'd get out of there if I were you. They're a little grumpy."

Taz looked around to see dozens of snakes hit the water, heading their way. "Fuck this." Taz and Hunter practically killed each other getting out of the small pond.

"Never seen a shifter walk on water before." Jared chuckled, giving Katrina a high five. "Good job."

"Thanks." She grinned at a glaring Hunter and scowling Taz. "I'd stay out of the water for a while, boys." She gave them a finger wave, then disappeared inside the house.

Taz spat blood on the ground, using his tongue to check the damage to his teeth. Only one felt loose.

"Are you okay?" Leda approached him, then leaned over to look into his face. With a frown and curse, she went over and punched Hunter in the stomach.

"Hey!" Hunter bent over. "What the hell?"

"I love him," she growled at Hunter. "Dumbass."

Taz grinned, then saw the tears of hurt in Leda's eyes. Anger surfaced quickly at her pain. He reached over and pulled her to him. His eyes sought Garrett as Taz walked toward him, Leda by his side.

"We are mated," he said as he stopped in front of Garrett, his eyes nor his voice wavering. "Nothing you do or say will change that. I should have done it the correct way, by asking your permission, and for that, I apologize. That's the only thing I will apologize for. I knew from the first time I met her that I would be mated to her. Last night was unexpected."

Taz paused, looking every single person there in the eye, leaving Hunter for last. "I wouldn't change it for the world, and I definitely will not let anyone here or anywhere insinuate what we did as adults is anything other than pure and true."

Jill sighed loudly, her hand to her chest, as did Ross, Emily, and Katrina, who had come back outside in time to hear what Taz had to say.

"I love Leda. I will cherish her more than my own life." Taz's eyes narrowed slightly. "Having your blessing means a lot to her. As my former alpha, it means some-thing to me. But as a man, I don't give a fuck either way."

Everyone but Garrett cringed at his last words. Garrett's eyes went to Leda. "You feel the same way?"

Leda's chin rose as she leaned closer to Taz. "I do."

Garrett nodded, but his eyes also narrowed, matching Taz's. "Know that if you ever hurt her, I will hunt you down and kill you slowly."

"I wouldn't expect anything different." Taz reached his hand out and waited for Garrett to take it.

Finally, Garrett shook Taz's hand, then held his arms out for Leda. "As long as you're happy, I approve."

"Thank you." She hugged him tightly.

"Okay, now that the butt-pucker moment is over, can we eat?" Steve announced, jumping down and hugging Leda. He shook Taz's hand. "Hurt her and I will eat you and spit you out."

Marcus was next with a warning of his own. "Treat her wrong, expect me to show up, fucker." He shook Taz's hand, then hugged Leda. "Congrats."

Hunter walked up, dripping wet, blood dribbled from his nose. "Hurt her and you know what's coming from me," he growled as he shook Taz's hand, then hugged Leda tightly, getting her clothes wet. He laughed. "That's for scaring the shit out of us, disappearing and hooking up with this dipshit. Congrats."

"Welcome to the family." Janna walked up and gave them both a hug. "They like you. They just have a weird way of showing it," she teased, then wrapped her arms around Garrett as they disappeared inside the house.

As soon as everyone had their say, Taz and Leda found themselves alone.

"Regretting me now?" Leda whispered, looking uncomfortable and a little embarrassed.

He clipped her chin gently, raising her eyes toward him. "Babe, I would walk through Hell for you. This was nothing, and something I expected." He kissed her softly. "The only regret I have is we have to wait until tonight for me to have you again."

A large smile spread across her face as she glanced toward the house. "I know a place."

Taz chuckled with a shake of his head. "You're trying to get me killed, aren't you?"

Before she could answer, they heard an excited yell from inside the house. The back door opened and out ran Sam. "I knew it!" He ran toward them. "Ma-ma-mates! Now I ha-ha-have a brother."

Sam tackled Taz, who fell dramatically and rolled around on the ground with the kid he was becoming attached to. They were his family now, and nothing would ever change that.

CHAPTER 21

$\mathcal{A}$llen Kingsman stared at his smoldering house, ignoring the bodies rotting all around him. His eyes shifted downward, spotting what looked like a wig and frame of some kind. He took a step while his eyes once again refocused on what used to be not only his home but his operation that was just getting off the ground. His brother's money was almost gone, and he needed another source of income. Stolen goods were a perfect source of fast cash.

With a curse, he looked down to see a short blonde wig laying over a frame. Using his boot, he pushed the thing aside. To say he was shocked was an understatement. His eyes widened as he stared at the image of his niece. "No." He couldn't believe she could do this, but obviously she, or someone who wanted him to believe it was her, had just turned his fucking world upside down.

"All the houses are empty," Bailey said, coming up

behind Allen. "But I found this asshole sleeping one off in the Watkins's house."

Allen turned to see Bailey pushing Minor toward him. "What in the fuck happened to my house?"

"She set it on fire." Minor pushed back at Bailey with a growl. "And took everyone. Killed our guys. It was a clusterfuck."

"And you didn't call the fire department?" Allen slapped Minor across the face, twice. "Are you a fool?"

"I didn't think you'd want the cops here." Minor rubbed his cheek.

Allen cursed as he glared at Minor. He had a fucking point. He didn't want the cops anywhere near here. "She didn't do this alone. Who helped the little bitch?"

"Those VC Warriors were with her, and the Lee County wolf pack." Minor's eyes widened. "One of the Warriors is the one who set the house on fire with his fucking hand. I about shit myself. They killed all of them." Minor looked around the ground.

Allen let that sink in. Jesus, she'd gotten the Warriors involved. She must be serious.

Suddenly, a smile spread across his face. Jason's little bitch wanted a fight? Well, she was about to get one, and the great thing about that was he wouldn't have to pay out fifty thousand dollars of his brother's money. He'd collect her life himself.

"How in the hell did you survive?" Allen asked, looking around at his dead men.

"He probably ran like the little pussy he is," Bailey sneered, giving Minor a look of disgust.

"I had to stay alive to let Allen know what happened," Minor defended.

"Was her brother with her?" Allen asked. Seeing Minor's confusion, he sighed. Minor hadn't been around that long, and the only reason Allen kept him was that the idiot would do anything he asked of him. "A kid. Did she have a little kid with her?"

"No." Minor shook his head. "But Malcolm was helping her, and so was my bitch, Jamie."

Rage overtook Allen's senses as he stared at Minor. Nothing pissed him off more than someone who wasn't loyal. Yeah, he knew that was hypocritical of him, but fuck it. His brother always treated him like shit, and Allen never had any loyalty for the asshole. Fuck him. Jason had stolen the woman he loved right out from under his nose. Jewel should have been his. But as soon as she'd seen Jason, he'd lost her. And yet, Allen still loved her to this day.

Yeah, he'd killed her, but that was more for his brother's benefit. Plus he knew that after killing Jason, she would never have forgiven him, so once again he'd thought, fuck it, and ended her life. He still had a part of her out there somewhere, and he would find him, raise the boy as he should be raised. Sam was a part of him, and he'd be damned if the Lee County fuckers would raise his son or his brother's daughter, Leda, the bitch.

The night he had approached Jewel with a deal that he would leave Kingsman was a night he would never forget. The image of Jewel naked underneath him as he fucked her hard would never leave him. He had kept his deal for years. Once she gave him her body for one night, a night that still made his dick hard at the memories, he'd left the pack. He would have given her the world if she just would have loved him and not his brother.

Turning, Allen glared at the house, then walked closer. It honestly wasn't the house. It was the bedroom where he had fucked her over and over again while his brother was out on a hunt. Toward the end, he had known she had started to like it. Her body had started defying her mind and heart as it moved against his, begging for his touch.

Reaching down, he adjusted his cock that stirred in his pants. He had kept that bedroom untouched; only he could enter it. Why? He didn't know. Morbid? Probably. Maybe it was because he had wanted everything his brother had, his wife included. But nothing was given to him, he took it. All of it without remorse.

"Fuck!" Allen bellowed, then kicked a burnt piece of wood. Taking a closer look, he frowned and bent over. *Holy shit.* "Minor, get your sorry ass over here."

"What, boss?" Minor stopped beside him.

"Get down in that hole and tell me what you see in the basement." Allen pointed toward the hole. "Hurry the fuck up."

Minor reluctantly wedged himself down there and then yelled as he dropped. "Dammit!"

"What do you see?" Allen called down through the hole.

"Not much. It's fucking dark," Minor called back. "Hold on, let me use my lighter." There was a small pause. "Hey, nothing's really burnt down here. A few things where the floor fell through, but it doesn't look bad."

"Go find a rope," Allen told Bailey as he started to lower himself into the basement. "If we're lucky, none of our shipments got ruined."

Allen dropped, landing easily on his feet. Seeing Minor's lit lighter, he headed that way and was relieved to see all the boxes but a few untouched. Heading farther down where light shone through, he glanced around to gauge where he was when he saw a large hole in the wall.

"What the fuck?" He frowned and then stopped, shocked. He knew exactly what this was. He looked around the floor to see things broken and scattered on the ground, items that were on the shelves that used to be there. Glancing up, he saw what remained of the shelves on the ceiling, with a strap handle at the bottom. Reaching up, he started to pull it down until it began to fall apart, so he let it go, but he finally understood the truth of something that had always made him wonder. "That son of a bitch."

Allen went farther until he stood just inside the hole. He fumbled for his own lighter in his pocket and flicked it, moving it around to see a door that had been left open, he assumed deliberately. Leda wanted him to see it, made damn sure he would see it.

He moved the lighter around, spotting the lights at the top of the tunnel.

"Wow, did you know this was there?" Minor stood behind him, using his own lighter to look around. "That's pretty cool."

"Yeah, real fucking cool." His shadowed face was a mask of rage. "I want every fucking member here in the next hour, and tell them to bring their friends."

Minor rushed out to do as he'd been told while Allen continued to look at his brother's work and what Leda had left open for him to find. This was how she'd escaped with his son. "Oh, I see it, little girl," Allen hissed. His lighter went out. "And I will be seeing you very soon." His voice rumbled in the darkness.

Allen stood in front of his destroyed home staring out at his pack. They'd survived the fray, as he'd given them a night off to kick back before heading back to Kingsman. None of them were happy with being called back from their partying and fucking whores to find their town empty and the main house of the alpha burned to the ground.

"As you see, we have all suffered a personal attack," Allen began, his voice ringing out so everyone could hear him. "This attack was instituted by my little bitch of a niece, who had help from the VC Warriors and Lee County wolves."

A murmur went through the crowd, which Allen expected. "In one hour, I am leaving for Lee County to avenge the wrong that has been done to this pack, our home. Who is with me?"

There was a moment of hesitation, but soon agreements to follow him rang out.

Allen wasn't certain how this would go with the vampires being involved. Most alphas wouldn't blink going after another pack, even the Lee County bastards, but the pack who followed him were loyal to him and rarely cared who they had to kill. It's why he'd welcomed them into his pack.

He held up the picture Leda had left for him. "I want her alive, and brought to me. I don't care what it takes, I don't care who you have to kill to get it done, but I want her alive. There will be a bonus for the man who achieves this, and believe me, I have a feeling she will be heavily guarded."

"What's the plan?" someone in the back shouted.

Looking around at them all, he smiled and then laughed loudly. "The plan, my friends, is to kill as many mother-fuckers as we can."

"That would be a big mistake," a voice said through the crowd.

"Malcolm!" Allen grinned without having to look around. He knew exactly where the bastard had been. "I was told you betrayed me."

Laughing, Malcolm glanced at Minor, who was standing near Allen. "By who, Minor?" Malcolm shook his head. "He's an idiot. I know where they are, how many there are, but more importantly, I can hand Sam to you. So is that your plan? Ride in and kill them?"

Allen stepped off what was left of his porch steps and

walked toward Malcolm, shaking his head. "You really think I'm that stupid? Minor may be an idiot, but he's loyal. You were loyal to my brother. I've always known that and have never trusted you." Allen stopped in front of Malcolm and tilted his head. He reached to grab Malcolm's phone. Looking down at it, he tsked, holding it up. "Who were you streaming this to? Jamie? A Warrior? Leda?"

Malcolm didn't answer; he just stared at Allen with hate. "You're going to lose."

"Oh no, *you're* going to lose, and so are they." Allen nodded as four men grabbed Malcolm, dragging him away. "Rough him up a little, but keep him alive."

Allen held the phone up and smiled at the red recording light. "Oh, Leda, you have truly fucked up," Allen said. "You should have stayed in your hole and not played with the big boys. See you soon. And to the bastards who killed my men—payback's a bitch."

Allen tossed the phone to Minor. "Send this to your whore," Allen ordered as he turned his back to walk away. "I want them to know exactly who is coming for them."

CHAPTER 22

*T*ension was high, and the mood around the pack became subdued as they waited for retaliation from Leda's uncle. They all knew it was coming. Early that morning, it was discovered that Malcolm had disappeared. No one knew where he had gone, not even Jamie.

Taz was short-tempered and pissed the fuck off. For that son of a bitch to slip out without any of them knowing was his fault. He should have kept a closer eye on him, but he had failed. He didn't take failure well, especially when it could deeply affect the people he cared about. He left Leda at Garrett's as he ran the perimeter, looking for any signs of trespassers.

There was nothing.

"Jamie hear from him yet?" Steve ran toward him, his usual carefree attitude not present.

"No, not that I've heard. She promised to let us know." Taz frowned, slowing for Steve to catch up. "I should have tied the fucker up."

"You think he went back to Kingsman?" Steve asked, but by his tone, that was what he thought.

"Yeah," Taz growled, taking the steps to Garrett's two at a time. "I do."

After opening the door, they walked inside. Everyone stood around while Dell held up a phone. Jamie stood with Devon, her eyes wet with tears.

"What's going on?" Taz immediately searched for Leda. She wedged her way toward him.

"Minor sent Jamie a video." Dell frowned. "We now know where Malcolm disappeared to." He hit Play, and Malcolm's voice filled the room.

"Jamie, I want you to show this video to everyone. I'm back at Kingsman. I know Allen will be back today, and I want to prove to everyone who I am loyal to. Even in a moment of weakness..."

"No!" Leda whispered, her voice filled with emotion as she moved closer to the phone.

"...deep in my heart, I knew I would never turn Leda over to Allen. Yes, I thought about it, but I know now I would never have done it. I'm going to find out their plan and let you know. Wait!"

Malcolm stopped talking, but they could hear him walking and then a faint voice. Instantly, Leda stiffened next to Taz. He knew exactly who the voice belonged to by her actions.

"What's the plan?" a voice came over the phone.

"The plan, my friends, is to kill as many motherfuckers as we can."

"That would be a big mistake." Malcolm's voice boomed throughout the room, but all they could see was the ground.

"Malcolm! I was told you betrayed me."

Malcolm laughed loudly. *"By who, Minor? He's an idiot. I know where they are, how many there are, but more importantly, I can hand Sam to you. So is that your plan? Ride in and kill them?"*

Taz and Dell's eyes met. Jared left the room with his phone to his ear.

"You really think I'm that stupid? Minor may be an idiot, but he's loyal. You were loyal to my brother. I've always known that and have never trusted you." The phone made a loud rustling sound. *"Who were you streaming this to? Jamie? A Warrior? Leda?"*

Fierce rage straightened Taz's back as he heard the bastard say her name. She reached over and squeezed his hand.

"You're going to lose." Everyone in the room could hear the hatred in Malcolm's voice.

"Oh no, you're going to lose, and so are they." The sound of struggle and curses echoed around them as they all remained quiet, listening and watching the

phone in Dell's hand. *"Rough him up a little, but keep him alive."*

Allen's face appeared on the screen, and Leda gasped, stepping back into Taz. *"Oh, Leda, you have truly fucked up. You should have stayed in your hole and not played with the big boys. See you soon. And to the bastards who killed my men—payback's a bitch."*

His face disappeared, but his voice still played. *"Send this to your whore,"* Allen ordered. *"I want them to know exactly who's coming for them."*

The room remained quiet, and Taz could feel the tremor in Leda's hand. "He'll kill him," she whispered, and they both looked at Jamie, who held onto Devon.

"Is th-th-tha-that Uncle?" Sam's shaking voice filled the room. Taz cursed as he spotted the boy standing in the doorway. Wide eyes in his pale face searched for a monster in the room. "Leda!" he cried out.

"I'm here, Sam." Leda rushed toward him and slid to her knees. "It's going to be okay. You're going to be fine."

Sam's tear-filled eyes stared at Taz over Leda's shoulder. His chin trembled uncontrollably, his fear evident to everyone in the room. "Don't le-le-let him hur-hur-hur-hur—" Sam closed his mouth and swallowed hard. "—hurt us, Taz."

"Never, buddy," Taz swore to the little boy who stared at him like a hero, but Taz didn't feel like a hero at the moment.

He glanced at Garrett, whose face was a mask of rage. "We need to get them out of here." Leda and Sam were his only concern, and he'd be damned if he let them down.

~

Leda heard Taz and stiffened. "Emily, can you take Sam to his room for a minute?" She begged Emily with her eyes. "Please."

"Of course." Emily rushed over, but Sam wouldn't let her go.

"No!" he refused, using just that one word. Leda knew his fear was making it hard for him to talk, and that's when he went to using one-syllable words.

"I promise you I'm not going anywhere." She pried his little arms from around her neck. "Go with Emily, and I'll be right there. I promise, Sam. Take Pepper with you."

Sam finally let go and called Pepper by snapping his fingers once. He looked toward Taz, and so did Leda. Taz gave Sam a nod. Leda turned to see Sam disappear up the steps with Emily.

Once she heard the door close, she turned to look at Taz. "I'm not going anywhere."

"Leda." Taz shook his head with a sigh. "You are not staying here. You and Sam need to—"

"Payback's a bitch," her uncle's voice said as Steve watched the video.

"What is he, a girl?" Steve snorted, his eyes narrowed on the screen. "Seriously, no one says that anymore."

"What in the hell are you doing?" Jill sighed, glaring at him. "And girls don't say that either."

"I've counted twenty guys." Steve looked up at everyone. "I've watched it twice. Malcolm definitely did us a solid with this video."

"We can't depend on that being the correct count." Slade was behind Steve, also watching the video. "But at least that gives us a starting count."

"Everyone is on their way." Jared walked back in. "What did I miss?"

"The asshole warning us that payback's a bitch." Steve chuckled, shaking his head.

"What? Is he a girl?" Jared frowned with no concern for the warning.

"That's what I said." Steve gave Dell the phone back.

"Marcus, go talk to the Kingsman and let them know what's going on. Anyone who wants to leave is free to do so. We'll make sure they have somewhere safe to go until this is over."

"Janna and the babies are leaving," Garrett announced, then looked toward Ross. "I think you should also, and Emily."

Hunter started to open his mouth, but a scream from outside stopped him.

"When did that video arrive?" Taz glanced at Jamie.

"As soon as it came, we rushed over here." Devon

frowned, his eyes filled with anger. "They waited to send it until they were close."

"They waited," Taz agreed. "Fuck!"

"Smart." Jared rushed toward the front of the house. "Soon to be dead, but smart."

Dell walked toward the window and looked out. Leda tried to see, but too many huge bodies blocked her way. "Warriors, spread out through the back." Dell opened the door. "Wolves, follow me. Women, stay put."

Leda finally was able to see out the window but was careful to stay out of sight for now. She didn't see anything at first, but then farther down the street, she saw a man staggering down the road. It was Malcolm.

"Oh no!" Jamie cried, her hand going to her mouth.

"Come on." Ross took her arm, leading her back to the kitchen. "The guys will get him. He'll be okay."

Leda and Ross shared a look. He didn't look okay.

Seeing movement, she watched as Mr. Watkins rushed out to help Malcolm. "No!" She knew the older man couldn't hear her, but she also knew it was a trap.

"Leda!" Her uncle's voice echoed up the street as if he were on an intercom. "Answer me, bitch, or you'll regret it!"

A gunshot made her jump, and she waited for Mr. Watkins to hit the ground, but it was Malcolm who fell face first onto the road. "Oh God." She panicked as she looked toward Taz. He had scattered with the others, and she couldn't see him.

"You have three seconds to appear in this street, or Burt here is going to leave Mrs. Watkins a widow. Now I know you don't want that on your pretty little head, niece. One!"

Leda glanced behind her at Janna and Ross. "Hide Sam."

"Two!" His voice grew louder. "Come on, Leda. The way you came into my pack and burned my house down, I thought you had bigger balls than this."

She turned to look at Jill, who had stayed behind to protect the women. "Don't do it," she warned Leda.

"If Taz gives chase, you stop him," Leda ordered, but when Jill shook her head, Leda got in her face. "Stop him. Swear it. I would do it for you if it were Slade."

"Dammit!" Jill cursed, then gave her a dirty look. "You are going to owe me big for this one."

Just as she headed out the door, she saw Taz step out. Fear like she never felt before hit her and sent her out the door faster than she'd ever moved in her life.

"Leda!" Taz yelled as he started to give chase, but was slammed back as if he'd run into an invisible wall. He glanced toward the house to see Jill staring at him with her hands out toward him. "What are you doing?"

"I'm sorry!" was all she said.

"Damn you!" Taz fought to free himself, but it was no use. He watched as Leda ran as fast as she could, putting herself in front of the older man. "No! Let me go!"

Leda heard Taz cursing and fighting to get free, but she would deal with that later, if she survived.

"I'm here, you son of a bitch!" Leda yelled, then moved back as a truck came barreling toward them with more than twenty men running behind it. Her uncle stood in the back of the pickup with a bullhorn.

He gave her a sinister smile. "Yes, there you are." He pointed his gun at her. "You know how easy it would be to end you right now?"

"A coward's way is usually pretty easy," she shot back. "Let Mr. Watkins go."

"You aren't giving the orders now," he sneered, then pulled the trigger. The shot went wide, but she felt the breeze of the bullet. She could hear Taz's bellow and cursing behind her.

"Someone you know, I take it." Her uncle aimed the gun toward Taz, who was totally out in the open and just standing there staring at her.

"What do you want, you bastard?" Leda hissed as she walked straight up to the truck, slamming her hand on it. "You want me? Here I am." She spread her arms wide.

"You have more fight than your father ever did." Allen lowered the gun. "I have to respect that about you, at least. I think you have more of your mother in you."

Leda didn't say anything to that. She just stood at the front of the truck, glaring up at her uncle.

"Where's Sam?" His face completely turned, and she witnessed the evil intent in his eyes.

"He's not here," Leda lied, then gave him a sinister grin.

"I'm not stupid either, *Uncle*." She mimicked his words from the recording.

"Yes, actually, you are." He aimed the gun at her. "I don't need you to find my son. Now that you're dead, there is nothing keeping him from me. I will tear this town apart, and I will find him. Goodbye, Leda. Tell your mother I said hello."

Sadness filled her soul as she slowly closed her eyes. The last thing she heard was Taz screaming her name in the distance.

CHAPTER 23

*T*az watched the bastard pull the trigger, but nothing happened. Only a loud click reverberated through the street.

"Ah, damn!" Allen sighed dramatically, then pulled out another gun. "Wrong one." He looked around the seemingly empty town. "This is for the Warriors and wolves hiding among us. Oh, I know you're there," Allen said through the bullhorn. "I'm going to take Leda with me. If anyone does anything to me or my men, I will kill her, for real this time. I want Sam."

Taz tried to take a step forward, but it was no use. He glared at Jill, but she refused to look his way.

"I was going to kill you all for killing my men, but honestly, I don't give a fuck." Allen's crazed laugh echoed through the bullhorn. "Count yourselves lucky, because next time, you won't be. I will kill you and then come after your family, your friends. Hell, I'll come after your fucking dogs. I'm a Kingsman."

Taz watched as each and every Warrior and wolf made themselves known. Dell came forward, followed by Garrett, Hunter, and Marcus. He fell in step with them, doing everything in his power not to run toward Leda to shield her from this man. Her uncle was on edge, and it wouldn't take much to send him over.

Allen looked around at the large group of vamps and wolves surrounding him and his men. "Oh, what a scary-looking crew," Allen mocked before laughing for a long moment. His manic laughter cut off abruptly as his face morphed into anger. "Get in the truck, Leda."

"No," she whispered, but Taz heard her.

Dammit, Leda. He tried to break into her thoughts, but she was shut off.

"Why don't you climb off that truck with your men and do this the shifter way?" Dell called out, his voice strong and sure.

"Oh, okay." Allen smiled and acted like he was going to do just that, but stopped. "Only one problem with that. I don't want to do it that way, and I'm in control here."

Originally outnumbered by the Kingsman pack, Taz held back his smile at the sound of motorcycles. The rest of the Warriors had arrived.

"You sure about that?" Leda tilted her head up at him. "At least they're giving you a fighting chance. It was more than you gave your own brother and my mother. She hated you. You know that, don't you? I've read her journal. I know everything, and as soon as you get your ass handed to you, I'm going to the elders with all the information I have."

"Goddammit!" Taz hissed trying to move closer. "Stop taunting him," he said to Leda, as if she could hear him. If he made any moves, she could be shot. No way would he chance that. Maybe it was a good thing Jill was holding him back.

"Wrong information to share," Allen growled as he jumped out of the truck, strode up to her and hit her across the face. "Get in the fucking truck." Grabbing her arm, he dragged her with his free hand, the gun in the other.

"Now!" Dell yelled, and all hell broke loose.

Suddenly Taz was free from Jill's power as he ran toward Leda while Allen was trying to haul her to the truck. Seizing the bastard by the back of the neck, Taz slammed his face into the truck as he pulled Leda free. "Get to the house!"

Leda fell backward but screamed out a warning when someone appeared behind Taz. Turning, Taz started fighting him off, giving Allen a chance to go after Leda. Steve stepped in to take the guy down, giving Taz freedom to grab Allen.

"Don't think so, motherfucker." Taz hit him with an elbow across the face. "Doesn't feel good, does it?"

Allen roared with rage, slamming himself into Taz. He was bigger, but Taz was faster. He took Allen down with him but rolled, flipping Allen over his head. They both stood at the same time.

"So, you and my niece, huh?" Allen wiped blood from his nose and looked at his hand with a frown. "I don't like to bleed, you little shit."

Taz spun, his foot connecting with Allen's face. He didn't even respond to the bastard. All he could think of was the son of a bitch hitting Leda. Nothing could stop Taz from unleashing his rage. Allen didn't stand a chance; blow after blow, Taz was a man possessed.

"Stop, or I'll kill her." Those words penetrated Taz's brain when nothing else did. He stopped, his head turning slowly as his eyes focused on Minor with a gun under Jamie's chin.

An inhuman snarl escaped Taz's throat.

"Let him up." Minor jammed the gun hard, making Jamie cry out.

Slowly, Taz stood and moved away from Allen, who lay moaning on the ground. Glancing around, Taz saw the Warriors had things under control as well as the wolves, even some of the new pack members from Kingsman. These worthless motherfuckers were no match for them. He saw Leda staring wide-eyed at Minor and Jamie. No one moved other than Allen, who tried to stand.

"You bastard." Allen spat out blood and broken teeth. "I'll kill you."

Minor glanced toward Leda. "Get in the truck," he ordered her. When Leda didn't move, he screamed, "Do it, or I swear to God, I will blow her head off."

"Then what are you going to do, genius?" Jared called out as the Warriors and wolves moved closer. "You kill her, we kill you."

Taz glanced at Allen, who was still having trouble trying to stand. He'd fucked him up good. The satisfaction with that knowledge just wasn't there, though. He was far from finished with the son of a bitch. While Minor was busy looking toward Jared, Taz moved closer to Leda, but stopped when Minor snapped his attention back toward him.

"Stop moving!" he bellowed, then looked at Allen. "Get up, Allen."

"He's having a little trouble there, Minus," Hunter replied, then glanced at a grinning Sid.

"Good one." Sid gave him a thumbs-up, then looked toward Minor. "Hey, let me give you a little advice. I've seen this situation before, many times. You listening?"

Minor's gaze was going everywhere at once. "You're just trying to confuse me."

"Don't think you need help there, buddy." Jared snorted before clearing his throat. "Sorry. You need to listen to Sid here. He's seen a lot of shit, and he's trying to help you."

Sid snapped his fingers, getting Minor's attention from looking at all his comrades lying lifeless on the ground. "Hey, focus." Sid waited for Minor to look his way. "Now, as I was saying, I've seen this situation before. You aren't getting out of here with her or Leda. Let's just get that straight. Not happening. But you can get out of here alive."

"How?" Minor frowned, his eyes looking hopeful.

"Don't listen to him," Allen slurred as he finally sat up. "They're lyin—"

Taz lifted his leg and kicked Allen in the face, effectively shutting him up. Taz glanced back at Sid. "Continue." One thing was for sure—these Warriors could talk anyone out of anything by confusing the shit out of them.

"Let her go." Sid cocked his eyebrow at Minor with a shrug. "It's simple, really. Let her go, hand over the gun, and you live. Kill her, don't hand over the gun and piss us off more than we already are, you die."

"And it will be painful and drawn out," Hunter added with a fake shiver.

Just as Minor was starting to pull the gun away from Jamie's face, the door to Garrett's slammed open. Taz watched in horror as Minor pulled the gun away from Jamie, and swung it toward the noise as Sam came running out the door screaming Leda's name.

Taz heard the sound of the shot before he could reach Leda, who had started to run toward Sam. Time stood still as her body was slammed forward by the force of the bullet and she hit the ground hard.

"No!" Taz roared, turning to see Devon pulling Jamie out of Minor's grip as Sid, Jared, and Hunter grabbed him. He slid to his knees just as Slade got to her. "Leda!"

Slade ripped her shirt. The bullet had hit her shoulder, but as he turned her over, Taz saw the damage. He heard Slade tell him she would be fine, but he lost it.

Moving away from Leda, he watched Sam being carried back into the house by Ross. His head then snapped toward Minor, who stared at him, terrified.

Reacting on gut instinct, Taz gave way to his wolf and shifted with aggressive force. Sid and Jared pushed Minor toward him as Taz stalked that way slowly.

"It was an accident." Minor's teeth chattered, the scent of fear rolling off him in sickening waves. "I swear I didn't mean it."

Taz snarled with a shake of his head as he slowly stalked his way.

"Don't think he believes you," Hunter said as he also stepped out of the way. "You best shift. That's the last advice you'll be getting."

Minor stumbled backward. Deciding against Hunter's advice, he took off running. Taz continued on his slow, measured movements, giving him a head start, then leaped forward. Within seconds, he was on top of the son of a bitch, tearing him apart.

"Damn! Remind me not to piss off your wolf." Sid walked over after Taz was finished, peering down at what used to be Minor. "Hey, Jared, how about shredded roast beef for dinner? I've got a killer recipe."

Jared was also staring over at Minor's remains. "Sounds good to me, man."

"You guys are fucked up." Blaze passed by, shaking his head with a grin.

Taz heard them, but he was far from a teasing mood. Still in wolf form and with the taste of blood on his tongue, he had to keep his wolf under control. His eyes swung toward Leda. She was sitting up with Slade working on her, Steve behind her so she had something to lean against.

Allen stared at him, his face a swollen mess from Taz's earlier beating. This guy was nothing but a sick piece of shit. Taz stalked toward him and stopped close enough for Allen to see Minor's blood on his fur. Taz snarled, revealing long sharp teeth.

"He's my son." Allen pointed over Taz's shoulder where Sam had disappeared. "I just want my son."

Taz snapped at him before stepping back and shifting. Covered in blood, Taz knelt in front of Allen while Dell and Garrett walked up behind the bastard, who still remained on the ground. Taz's knee kick must have really fucked him up; he smiled at the thought.

"Sam is not your son, you sorry son of a bitch." Taz spat in the bastard's face. "He will know nothing about you beyond you being the uncle who killed his parents."

"No, you can't do that." Allen sluggishly reached for Taz, but Taz just knocked his hand away.

"No one tries to harm what's mine," Taz sneered. "But Leda is the one who has the right to finish you off. Count yourself lucky that you have more time."

"What?" Allen's swollen eyes opened a little wider.

"Oh, you heard me, fucker. Leda has the right to kill you because you killed her parents." Taz gave him an evil smile. "But secretly, I hope to hell she gives me that right, because my people, the Cherokee, know how to make someone suffer, and you will suffer greatly."

"You have the right." Leda's voice reached them, weak and yet strong in her own special way. "And I hope you rot in hell, *Uncle*."

Taz's sinister grin grew across his face. "I'll be right back." He walked over and knelt in front of Leda, his smile gone as he searched her eyes. "You okay?"

"Slade says I'll live." She reached out to touch him with her good arm, but he stopped her.

"Not while I have that bastard's blood on me."

"You're naked." She grinned, then hissed when she moved her shoulder.

"Yeah, dude," Steve said, looking away. "I don't want to see your junk, man. Get some clothes on and take care of that shit. I've got Leda until you get back. Though I'm bummed I'm going to miss it."

"I'll tell you all about it when I get back," Taz promised, then heard Allen whimper.

Standing, Taz stared down at Leda, who gave him a nod. "Go on. I'm fine. I just want this over."

"You sure she's okay?" Taz asked Slade.

"She's good," Slade replied as he stood. "Once she shifts, it should heal quickly."

Marcus tossed Taz clothes that he swiftly tugged on. He glanced at the truck. "The keys in there?"

Hunter ran over and jumped in the driver seat. "Yep."

Taz snatched Allen by the hair and dragged him to the truck. Jared and Sid helped Taz toss him in the back. Allen screamed in pain, the sound giving Taz a moment of satisfaction. Dell got in the front while Sid and Jared sat in the back with Taz.

"What?" Jared said when Sloan glared at them. "We ain't missing this shit."

Taz watched Leda, who was staring at him, until the truck disappeared. He then looked down at her silently crying uncle.

"Want me to knock him out?" Sid offered, but Taz shook his head.

"No. I want him alert for this." Taz ignored Allen's begging as they headed deep into the woods.

CHAPTER 24

*L*eda woke in wolf form, her head coming up quickly when she noticed it was dark outside. Shifting into human form, she glanced down at her shoulder, happy she was healing so quickly. There was hardly any pain. Sam lay a few feet away from her, no doubt afraid to leave her alone.

The Warriors had stayed and helped clean up the bodies, then assisted in deciding what to do with the survivors. It had all been foggy to her, but she'd been able to tell them all goodbye and thank them.

Slade had made her shift before he left with her promise that she would stay that way until she healed. Rolling her shoulder, she hissed when pain shot through her body.

"You shouldn't have shifted." Taz's voice came from the darkness.

Gasping, Leda carefully stood. "Taz, when did you get back?"

He reached out of the darkness as soon as she was close enough and carefully pulled her onto his lap. "I just got here a few minutes ago."

His hair was wet and his clothes smelled fresh. "You should have woken me."

"I like watching you in wolf form." He kissed her softly.

Leda pulled away to look at him. "Tell me."

"Leda, I don't want to—"

"I gave you my right." She stopped him. "I deserve to know, and after this, I don't ever want to mention his name again."

"He is still alive, barely." Taz sighed with hesitation. "It's something my people did back in the old days. You hang someone by their feet, cutting them in places on their body so they slowly bleed out. Unfortunately, an animal will probably get him before that happens, but he will suffer tenfold for what he put you and Sam through."

"What if he gets away?" Leda couldn't help the fear rushing to her chest at the knowledge he was still alive.

"I wouldn't have left him if I thought that was a possibility," Taz reassured her. "His Achilles are sliced, and no one has ever gotten out of my rope ties."

"Thank you," she whispered, laying her head against his chest, snuggling close.

"I need you to promise me something." Taz's voice

deepened with emotion. "Don't ever put yourself in danger like you did today. I understand what you did, but it wasn't and still isn't easy for me, knowing how close I came to losing you more than once."

"I know." Leda reached up, touching his cheek. "It's just that I was so afraid of someone getting hurt because of me. That's something I can't change."

"I don't want you to change, Leda," Taz whispered against her hand. "I just want you to be more careful with your life. That isn't too much to ask. I don't know what I would have done if something happened to you today. I can't lose you."

"I can't lose you either." She kissed him, then straddled his lap.

"You're naked," he said against her lips, repeating what she'd said to him earlier.

"I know." She grinned. "What are you going to do about it?"

Taz had never loved her more. He glanced around the room, somehow managing to tear his gaze away from the perfect woman on his lap. Sam was curled up a few feet away fast asleep. Holding Leda tightly, he stood and walked toward the door. Grabbing a cover on the way, he wrapped it around her. He hoped to hell they didn't run into anyone as he made his way through the house and outside.

Taz hoped he'd reassured her about her uncle. He'd

spoken the truth; Allen wasn't going to get away. He hadn't told her everything he had done to the bastard, but Jared and Sid had loved it. Even with all Allen's begging and screaming, Taz made sure he suffered just as he'd made Leda and Sam suffer for years.

When they'd returned, Jared and Sid had given Steve a play-by-play of events. He'd been spitting mad he hadn't gone with them to see Taz finish Leda's uncle.

"Damn, man," Steve had said with a large frown. "Next time I'm in town, we are going to find someone who needs to suffer, and this time I'm going."

Taz grinned at the memory and realized he had made a good friend with the goofy fucker. He was definitely someone Taz could count on, and he hoped Steve felt the same way.

"Where are we going?" Leda whispered as he continued to carry her toward the woods.

"Not far," he whispered back. Finding a secluded spot, he stopped. "Are you sure you're up to this?"

"Up to what?" she teased, then nipped at his lip.

He rubbed his hardness against her and chuckled when she moaned. He reached down and unbuttoned his jeans, then unzipped them. With a little work, he freed his hard cock. "Tell me if I hurt you, Leda," he said seriously. "I mean it. I don't want to hurt you."

"I don't think you could ever hurt me, Taz." Leda held onto him with her good arm. "But you're going to have to do a lot of the work."

"Babe, I'll do all the work just to be inside you." Taz knew she was ready for him; he could smell her need, her desire for him. With one swift motion, he sank her down on his cock, and they both groaned together.

Taz took it slowly, wanting them both to enjoy the sensations of each other's body. "I love you." He stared into her eyes and felt tears at the back of his. "I almost lost you today."

"But you didn't." She gave him a small smile. "I'm here, Taz. I will always be here for you."

They remained quiet as they got lost in each other. It was the most peaceful he had felt in such a long time. The way her body tightened around him, he knew she was close; he made sure this time they exploded together. Pumping harder and faster, he lost himself inside her. His eyes never left hers as he watched every second of pleasure she felt. It was as if he was looking into a mirror with his own pleasure matching hers.

Her mouth opened wide as a sexy moan escaped her lips. Her eyes widened as she stared up at him, and never in his life had he experienced such love as he witnessed in her gaze. His neck corded as he pushed himself as deeply inside her as he could and held her as she pulsed around his cock. Letting loose, he forced his eyes to remain open instead of closing them in total ecstasy. He wanted her to do the same. "Don't close those eyes." Taz pulled out and then slammed into her, but not enough to hurt her as more of him spilled inside her body.

She did as told, her nails digging into his arms as she

squirmed against him, seeking more of what he was giving her. Nothing had ever made him feel more like a man than that moment or more possessive over this woman, his woman, who clung to him.

He continued his loving assault on her body until he couldn't take any more. Letting himself go, he finally looked away as his head snapped back and a roar of pleasure escaped him. It was a mix of human and wolf.

"Oh, wow." Leda sighed, her breathing ragged. "I liked that… a lot."

"Noted." He gave her a wink, then slowly lowered her to her feet. After he wrapped the cover around her, he buttoned up his jeans.

"Listen, I know this is a little soon." Taz reached into his pocket. "And I'm not really sure how this is done…." He knelt in front of her.

Leda gasped at the simple diamond ring he held out.

"This was my mother's ring." He cleared the emotion from his throat. "She told me that one day I would find that special woman, and when I did, she wanted me to have something to give her. She would have loved you."

"It's beautiful, Taz," Leda cried as he took her hand.

"Leda Kingsman, I promise to put you first in every-thing, to give you anything you desire, and to love you unconditionally." Taz stared up at her. "You're already my mate, but that's not enough. I want you in every way there is to have you. Will you marry me?"

"Yes!" Leda laughed and cried as he slipped the ring on

her finger. Wrapping her arms around his neck, she kissed him.

"I want you and Sam to meet my sister," he said against her lips.

"I would love to meet her." Leda's smile was bright and made her teary eyes sparkle. She took a deep breath, her tone turning serious. "Thank you for being patient with me."

"You were worth the wait." Taz kissed her hard. There was no chance they'd be making it back to the house anytime soon, which was fine with him. He'd be a happy man to spend the rest of his life with Leda right here, naked with a quilt. Her wearing his mother's ring made everything perfect. For the first time in his life, he was content, and he had this beautiful woman to thank.

He glanced up at the sky and knew his mother was smiling down on them.

Taz walked deep into the woods, miles and miles from town. Malcolm was beside him. In a week, he had made a full recovery from being shot.

He knew Malcolm was nervous, but he had to give the guy credit; when Taz told him to come with him, he didn't question it. And even this far from town, Malcolm still didn't ask any questions.

"Holy fuck!" Malcolm gagged, glancing around. "What's that smell?"

"Allen," Taz said matter-of-factly as he tied a bandana around his lower face. He tossed one to a gagging Malcolm.

Seeing a dead Allen still hanging, he grinned and didn't hold back his chuckle when Malcolm stumbled backward.

"That's Allen?" Malcolm asked, shocked. When Taz nodded, an abrupt laugh burst from Malcolm. "Son of a bitch, that is fucking perfect. But what in the hell happened to him?"

"Bear most likely." Taz glanced at Allen's half-eaten rotten corpse. "My ancestors used this technique, and as you can see, it works really well. Grab some wood and pile it in that circle of rocks."

Taz climbed the tree and cut the rope with his sharp hunting knife. What remained of Allen fell to the ground. Jumping from the tree, Taz helped Malcolm and then started the fire. He used the rope to haul Allen onto the flames.

They walked away from the smell and hunkered down to make sure the fire stayed lit. Taz could feel Malcolm looking at him and smiled inside.

"Why did you bring me here?" Malcolm asked, curiosity and concern coloring his words.

Taz turned to look him in the eye. "I believe you did what you did because of your sister. I understand what one will do for family." Taz looked back to the fire. "That is what I do for family. Anyone who threatens my family or harms my family will meet such a fate as Allen. If they suffer, I will make sure the son of a bitch suffers ten times worse."

Malcolm nodded, then glanced back at the fire. "Good to know. You're one crazy son of a bitch."

They kept quiet until Malcolm glanced over at him again.

"I don't have feelings for Leda," Malcolm informed him. "Just wanted you to know that."

A large smile spread across Taz's face. "Good to know." He stood, confident the fire would remain inside the rocks. He clapped Malcolm on the back. "And yes, I am a crazy son of a bitch."

Two chapters were closed in that moment. Allen was literally no more, and Malcolm learned what could happen if he made one wrong move where Leda was concerned. It was a damn good day.

With an extra lightness in his heart, Taz turned away and headed home to his mate, to his future.

Made in the USA
Columbia, SC
15 January 2021